A KILLE   LY

"Mandy, you know none of this is true."

"He's a skunk, Mom! He's after your money now. You can't trust him. You have to tell him to leave this house."

"Mandy, I won't listen to any more of this slander about your stepfather. Do you hear me?"

Jumping to her feet, Mandy began to pace back and forth. "He's not my stepfather! Can't you see what he's doing?"

"That's enough!"

"Listen to me, Mom. You're in danger! He's a liar from hell, Mom. He's moving in for the kill. He had this boy, Jimmy Boatman, take stuff from my room. They're working together against me. I think he also had something to do with Dad's dea—"

Her mother stood suddenly. "Hello, Harlan. We were just talking about you."

Mandy sensed Kinsley's dark presence behind her. He moved around slowly, sliding next to her mother, putting a hand on her shoulder.

Kinsley had a worrisome twinkle in his eyes. "I hope you were saying good things about me."

———

This book also contains a preview
of the next exciting book in the
TERROR ACADEMY series by Nicholas Pine.

THE BOOK STORE
1032 STALKER AVENUE
SHEBOYGAN, WI 53081
PHONE 452-6640

TERROR ACADEMY
LIGHTS OUT

NICHOLAS PINE

B
BERKLEY BOOKS, NEW YORK

LIGHTS OUT

A Berkley Book / published by arrangement with
the author

PRINTING HISTORY
Berkley edition / June 1993

All rights reserved.
Copyright © 1993 by C. A. Stokes.
Material excerpted from STALKER by Nicholas Pine
copyright © 1993 by C. A. Stokes.
This book may not be reproduced in whole or in part,
by mimeograph or any other means, without permission.
For information address: The Berkley Publishing Group,
200 Madison Avenue, New York, New York 10016.

ISBN: 0-425-13709-0

A BERKLEY BOOK ® TM 757,375
Berkley Books are published by The Berkley Publishing Group,
200 Madison Avenue, New York, New York 10016.
The name "BERKLEY" and the "B" logo
are trademarks belonging to Berkley Publishing Corporation.

PRINTED IN THE UNITED STATES OF AMERICA

10 9 8 7 6 5 4 3 2 1

This book is dedicated to
Vanessa and Jessica Simm,
The Potato Sisters

ONE

Mandy Roberts stood on tiptoe on the end of the diving board, carefully balancing there with her back to the smooth surface of the swimming pool. Her slender five foot five inch frame quivered for a moment and then held a steady pose in the black one-piece bathing suit. Green eyes concentrated on something in the distance as she focused. A bright spring sun brought out the reddish streaks in Mandy's shoulder-length brown hair, making her look like a beautiful Olympic athlete about to go into competition.

Her father, Vernon Roberts, called to her from the barbecue grill. "Come on, Mando! You can't stand there all day."

Her friends, Steve and Tara, were also watching intently. Steve told her to "go for it," while Tara bit her fingernails. They both wanted her to execute the dive, especially after Mandy had boasted that she was brave enough to try a back flip with a twist.

So far, Mandy had performed the diving maneuver only once. No one had been watching on that attempt. Her heart pounded and she was a little weak in her knees. What if she belly-flopped in front of the four most important people in her life?

Mandy's mother, a statuesque blonde, was laying on a chaise longue near the pool. She pulled down her sunglasses and gazed toward her daughter. "Honey, be careful. Don't hit your head on the board. Honey, don't—"

"Mom!" Mandy said. "I'm trying to concentrate!"

"Just be careful."

"Your mother's right," her father called. "Maybe you shouldn't—"

Mandy flexed her knees, bending forward slightly, dropping her hands and then raising them to gain momentum. Flying upward, she threw back her head, tossing the red-streaked tresses in a careless manner. She left the board and started to whirl in a complete circle. As she tucked into a tight ball, she saw the surface of the board coming at her head. If she didn't do something quickly, she was going to end up with a cracked skull!

"Mandy!" her mother cried.

When she opened herself out of the ball, Mandy twisted once and came down into the pool, missing the board by inches. Her body barely made a splash as she went in feet first. As soon as she surfaced in the cool water, she heard the others applauding.

"Good one," Steve said.

Tara told her to do it again.

Her mother shook her head. "You almost brained yourself, Mandy. Don't you—"

"Oh, Mom. I'm okay."

Mandy swam to the edge of the pool and lifted herself onto the tiled edge of the concrete rectangle. Her family was lucky enough to live in Prescott Estates, one of the best neighborhoods in Port City. Usually the pool wasn't used until late June, but unseasonably warm weather had arrived at the end of May, prompting her father to uncover the pool a little early.

Mandy turned her green eyes on Vernon Roberts, who stood at the barbecue grill turning hamburger patties. Mandy thought he looked sort of nerdy in his chef's hat, plaid shorts, gray T-shirt, ratty sneakers, and a purple apron that bore the inscription *Burger Busters*.

"It's almost ready," Mr. Roberts said. "Are you guys hungry?"

Mandy nodded, though she really hadn't worked off her breakfast. The late morning barbecue had been her father's idea. He was so thoughtful and kind.

"Nice dive," Mr. Roberts went on. "Are you going to try out for the diving team next year? You'll be a senior then."

Mandy grimaced and laughed. "Central doesn't have a diving team," she replied. "Just ask your friend Coach Chadwick, Dad."

Her father shrugged. "I could be the coach."

"You've got enough to do," Mandy replied. "Too much."

"Well, that's true. Darn! I think I need more hickory chips."

Mandy's father was a guidance counsellor and an English teacher at Central Academy. He also coached the golf team and was the faculty sponsor for the drama club. His extra jobs at school had allowed him to save enough money to buy the three-bedroom house with the pool. Her mother also worked, managing a small dress shop in Tremont Mall. Mandy was proud of her parents, her home, and her friends. Having them all together on such a gorgeous morning made her feel elated—but she knew her happiness might not last until the afternoon.

She glanced nervously at her father, trying to hide her apprehension. "What time are you leaving for school?" she asked.

Mr. Roberts looked at his watch. "It's quarter past eleven now. I have to be there at quarter to one."

Mandy frowned, wondering if she was ever going to get the chance to tell the awful news. "But the graduation ceremony doesn't start until two-thirty. Why do you have to leave so early?"

"I've got to check the PA system," he replied. "I'm the only one who knows how to work it."

How could she fault him for being so dedicated to school activities? He was always volunteering for duties that didn't pay any extra. Everyone, faculty and students, respected the lanky, intelligent counsellor with gray temples and a flashing smile. He was known as a good guy. He had even planned the morning barbecue for Mandy and her friends because they were only juniors and he didn't want them to feel left out during all the senior class commotion of graduation day.

"Get ready, kids," he called to Steve and Tara. "It's meat!"

Mandy stood up, straightening the seams of the black suit. She pushed her wet hair back, wishing she was a senior. She would get her chance after summer vacation. She wanted her last year at Central to be perfect.

Her mother glanced at her again, peering over the rims of the sunglasses. "Aren't you glad I talked you into a one-piece?"

Mandy made a face and shrugged. "I guess. I still liked the other one."

"It was too skimpy," her mother replied. "And it was Day-Glo orange!"

Barbara Roberts was wearing baggy shorts and a white polo shirt. She had blondish hair, and green eyes like her daughter. Sometimes Mrs. Roberts worked out at their club, but she was still able to maintain her figure even when she turned lazy and stopped exercising. Leaning forward in the chair, she grabbed something and tossed it to Mandy.

Mandy caught the bottle of sunscreen. "Thanks, Mom."

"I don't want you to burn," Mrs. Roberts replied.

Her father laughed. "Lest we not forget about

the depleted ozone layer. I think we're going to have a scorcher of a summer this year."

Mandy hesitated for a moment when she saw her mother reach for an open pack of cigarettes she'd kept neatly hidden in her shorts. "Mom! I thought you quit!"

Mrs. Roberts stuck the filter tip between her lips. "Well, I started back again, okay?"

"Mom! Those things cause cancer. I don't want—"

Mrs. Roberts shot her an angry look. "Don't start with me, Amanda!"

Mandy appealed to her father, whose clownish smile had disappeared. He seemed concerned about his wife. He nodded to Mandy as if to say, "I'll talk to her later." Mandy turned away from her parents and walked toward Steve and Tara, who lounged at the other end of the pool.

Steve Latham reclined on a folding beach chair. His hazel eyes watched longingly as Mandy approached. Steve had a crush on Mandy, though he had never told anyone. In the beginning stages of their relationship, Mandy had given him the "just friends" speech before he could even try to kiss her. It hurt that Mandy might never feel the same way about him, but he hung in there, hoping for a shift in the tide. He knew Mandy would go for a popular, jock-type, someone like Brett Holloway, who she had been dating for a couple of weeks. Brett was everything, while Steve was just a skinny, gangly, awkward kid with an ugly retainer on his teeth.

Tara Evans had been Mandy's best friend since kindergarten. She was petite with dark, curly hair, dark blue eyes, and a cute face. Tara had been dating a boy from the baseball team, but he had gone away for the summer to some baseball camp. She wasn't really mad about him, so she hadn't missed him much. Not yet, anyway.

"How was my back flip?" Mandy asked.

Tara stood and tossed her a towel. "Where'd you learn to dive like that?"

"I've been practicing," Mandy replied.

Tara nodded appreciatively. "You're braver than me. I have to hold my nose when I jump in feet first."

Steve took out his retainer and stuck it in the pocket of his loud red summer shirt. "When do we eat?"

Tara grimaced. "You're always hungry."

"Well at least I'm not named after a plantation in some stupid book," Steve replied. "Tara—*geez*!"

Tara put her hands on her hips. "Can I help it if my mother read *Gone With the Wind* three times before I was born?"

"You're lucky you didn't get stuck with Scarlett," Mandy said.

Steve said, "What did I hear about meat?"

Mandy gestured toward the grill. "Dad says it will be ready in a minute."

"Good," Steve said.

Tara gazed adoringly at Mr. Roberts. "Your father is way cool. I wish my dad was like him. My dad is always so—I don't know. He's not able to chill out like your father."

Mandy glanced over her shoulder. Her father was a special person. He seemed so stable, and happy most of the time. He had his moods like anyone else, but his disposition was peaceful as a rule. He could find the upbeat side of anything. Mandy hated to think that she might ruin his optimism with her bad news. How was she going to tell him?

Tara peered at her best friend. "What's wrong, Mandy?"

"Nothing. I'll tell you later."

Steve looked hurt. "Oh yeah, leave me out. It's a girl thing. Don't tell me, I don't want to know."

Mandy draped the towel over her shoulders and sat down on a marble bench. "I don't know—it's just, oh, so stupid. But I have to do it."

"Do what?" Tara asked impatiently as she eased back onto the lounger. "Tell me, Mandy. We haven't had any secrets since the third grade."

"It's lame," Mandy insisted. "I—I just don't want to hurt my father's feelings. He's so good to me."

Steve gazed toward Mrs. Roberts, who exhaled a billow of smoke. "Oh, I thought it was something to do with your mother. You two looked like you were gonna have a fight over there."

"I just want her to quit smoking," Mandy said. "But I'm worried about my dad right now. About what I have to tell him."

"What?" Tara demanded.

Mandy leaned back in her chair. "All right. This is it. You know I was named to be editor of the *Central Crier* this year."

"We were at the banquet," Tara replied. "I'm going to be editor of the art section and Steve is going to be Managing Editor. We'll have the best school paper in the county."

"Hush," Steve said. "Let her finish."

Mandy took a deep breath. She had been dying to tell someone. It was like trying to pull out a deeply buried splinter.

"I don't want to be editor of the school paper," she told them. "I never wanted that job."

Steve gaped at her. "No way."

Tara's big, dark eyes grew even wider. "Mandy! You can't do that. You'll break up the team. We're the Three Musketeers."

"You can work for whomever . . . or is it whoever? I never can remember. Anyway, you can work for someone else," Mandy said. "And I'm not quitting the paper; I just want to be a reporter, not an editor."

"Who's going to be editor and chief?" Tara asked.

Mandy pointed to Steve. "Latham can handle it. Can't you?"

Steve's countenance slacked into a thoughtful expression. "You might have a point there."

Tara pushed Steve's shoulder. "Stop it. You don't deserve to be editor and chief."

Mandy threw the towel at them. "Cool it. I told you, I don't want to be editor of that dopey paper.

I don't care how hard my father worked to get me the job. I—"

Tara straightened up suddenly and put her finger to her lips. "Shh. Here he comes."

They tabled their discussion as Vernon Roberts walked comically toward them with three paper plates balanced on his arms. The burgers were ready. The three of them forced smiles as he approached.

"Don't stop talking because of me," Mr. Roberts said. "Hey, check out the plates. I used to be a waiter in college. Anybody hungry? Steve? I hope you didn't eat a late breakfast. I mean, we had to get this going early because I have to be at school for the graduation ceremony."

"It's find, Dad," Mandy said. "Thanks a lot."

"Sure," Tara echoed. "Thanks."

Mr. Roberts offered a plate to Tara. "Guests first. Tara, you take cheese, pickle, and mustard."

Tara grabbed the plate. "How did you remember that?"

"I'm a genius, eh," he replied. "Either that or the fact that I've been serving you hamburgers since you were six years old."

Steve eyed the fresh food. "Looks good, sir."

"Let me see," Mr. Roberts went on. "Steve, you're cheese, mustard, mayo, onion, relish, double tomato, lettuce, pickles, and sauce on a sesame seed bun."

Steve reached for the plate. "Solid, Mr. R. How did you know?"

Mr. Roberts raised one eyebrow and made a

goofy face like a silent film comedian. "I've seen you eat. There's more if you want seconds."

Steve offered his thanks but it came out "Fmanks," because he had already bitten into the burger.

"Easy, big fellow," Mr. Roberts teased. "Don't hurt yourself."

Tara threw a napkin at Steve. "Gross! You're not supposed to wear it, Latham. Wipe your chin."

Mandy felt obligated to defend her guest from the joking. "He just likes to eat. He's a healthy growing boy."

Tara laughed. "He's an animal."

Steve just kept eating. At six foot two, he was one of the taller kids in the junior class. He was also one of the lightest at a hundred and thirty pounds. He needed to put on some weight.

"A plain cheeseburger for my daughter," Mr. Roberts said to Mandy. "You're a wild child, Mando. A party animal. The next thing you know, you'll be drinking soda!"

Mandy blushed a little. Her father had grown up in the sixties. He was always telling Mandy to lighten up some, not to take everything so seriously. Mandy kept reminding him that it was now the nineties. Some things had to be taken more seriously.

Their discussions always ended with Mandy getting flustered, but her father gradually got her laughing again. The other kids at school loved Mr. Roberts's funky style. He had helped a lot of Central graduates find their true paths. Mandy just didn't want to have one of those discussions in front of Steve and Tara.

Steve looked up from his burger. "I'll take a soda."

Mrs. Roberts brought a Coke to Steve and then went back to her chair. Steve washed down the burger and started on the chips. How could he stay so skinny? Tara wondered.

Mr. Roberts turned to Mandy. "I thought Brett Holloway was coming over."

Steve froze for a moment, almost choking. He didn't want Brett Holloway at the gathering. Although Mandy had been dating Brett, they weren't connecting, much to Steve's delight. He recovered quickly, eating the pickle and the scraps of lettuce, sure that none of them had noticed his pause.

Tara gazed dreamily toward the clear New England sky. "You're so lucky, Mandy. Brett is a hunk."

Mandy glared daggers at Tara. She didn't want *this* kind of boy-talk to take place in front of her father. Mr. Roberts pretended not to hear Tara.

Mandy glanced down into the pool. "Brett had to go to the gym this morning. Coach Chadwick called him in."

Vernon Roberts studied his daughter, wondering why she and Brett hadn't really clicked. They were the perfect type to go steady, become childhood sweethearts, get married in college and have a family by their early twenties. Of course, it was clear to a father's eyes that Steve was crazy about

Mandy, though it was not his place to say anything. Mandy had to learn things on her own. He had taught her to be an independent, clear-thinking girl. She had rarely been a disappointment to her parents.

Mandy was quiet for a moment. She thought about Brett. It had really crushed her that Brett had missed her party. They had only been dating a short while. Brett had been a perfect gentleman—so far. He *was* a total hunk—sandy hair, broad chest, kind brown eyes. Mandy just wanted to take things slowly. There were certain decisions—mainly about going steady—that Mandy wasn't ready to make yet. Brett would just have to wait.

Mr. Roberts snapped his fingers, trying to make the situation better but only making it worse. "That's right, they're electing the new captain of the swim team today. Coach Chadwick told me the former captain is graduating."

"Team captain," Tara said enviously. "Brett's a co-captain on the football team, too."

"Mr. Perfect," Steve said in a jealous tone.

"Just think," Tara went on. "You'd be going steady with the biggest jock in the school."

Mandy glared at her overly talkative friend. "We're not going steady!"

Tara grinned. "Not yet."

Steve rose to get another burger from the grill. The mention of Brett Holloway made him ravenous. Brett, Mr. Central Academy, the All-American Boy. Steve was only the vice-president of the skating club and an editor on the *Crier*. There wasn't much mystery about who Mandy would pick to be her boyfriend. It was a lock for Brett.

Steve looked at Mr. Roberts. "Er, I hate to say it, but your burgers are burning, sir."

Mr. Roberts jumped to his feet, waving his spatula like a broadsword in a Shakespearean tragedy. "A burger, a burger, my kingdom for a burger. I'll save them!"

Everyone laughed but Mandy. She looked dolefully at her paper plate. She wasn't hungry.

How was she going to break the news to her father? He had pulled some strings to get her the job as the editor and chief of the *Central Crier*. But Mandy had never said that she *wanted* to be head of the paper. She just wanted to be a reporter.

Tara met Mandy's fretful gaze. "Are you okay?"

Mandy nodded. She hated to hurt her father's feelings. She had special relationships with both her parents. Vernon and Barbara Roberts had always put the truth first. They had taught Mandy to think for herself.

Dream parents, Tara thought, especially Vern Roberts and his wacky sense of humor.

"How can I tell him?" Mandy asked in a low voice. "He took ice cream bars to Mrs. Wilkins for a month to bribe her into giving me the top job at the *Crier*. He thought I wanted it. He's never done anything like that before, Tara."

"It'll be all right," Tara said sympathetically.

"Besides, Mrs. Wilkins would have chosen you anyway. You're the best editor we have, Mandy."

Mandy grimaced. "No, I'm not the best. Not even close. As an editor, I'm average. But I know I'm a good reporter."

Tara did not argue. Mandy could write and take her own pictures. She was good at anything she tried—when she *chose* to try.

"Dad thinks I can be a hotshot editor some day," Mandy went on. "But I want to be a writer."

Tara leaned back, drifting off into a daydream. "I can see it now. You and Brett—married. He's a pro athlete and you're a gossip columnist. You both live in New York. They send you to do a story on the—"

Mandy waved at her. "Stop it. I'm not even sure I like Brett. And I know I want to do more than write gossip columns."

Tara slipped back to reality. "When are you going to tell your dad?"

Mandy sighed. "I'm not sure. Maybe before the ceremony. It might be better just to go ahead and get it over with."

"It's not that bad," Tara insisted. "You think he'll get mad at you?"

Mandy shook her head, frowning. "He doesn't get mad, he gets hurt. Then he sulks and pouts until he gets over it. Oh, I know it's not the end of the world, but if I hurt his feelings, I'll think it's all my fault."

"Just tell him. You'll feel a lot better when you do."

Mandy glanced over at her father, who was spooning a burger onto Steve's plate. He seemed so happy and carefree. He was a bit like Merlin, the magician for King Arthur. He worked magic sometimes. He had talked Mrs. Wilkins into making Mandy editor of the paper.

Maybe she should wait until after the ceremony to tell him.

No! She had to stand up for what she wanted.

What if she spoiled the whole day?

Or the entire summer?

Everything came down to what her parents had taught her. Be your own person. Fight for what you believe. Don't surrender. Take pride in yourself. Face adversity head on.

She had to tell him.

TWO

"Dad?"

Mandy stood under the archway that framed the entrance to the living room of the Roberts's Victorian-style house. Her father, who had his hand on the front doorknob, turned to smile at her. Mandy thought she was going to cry for a moment, but she told herself to hold back the tears.

"Dad, I—"

"What is it, honey?"

Mr. Roberts had changed into a white dress shirt, a pair of brown trousers, and a solid black tie. The sneakers were gone, replaced by a pair of shiny brown wing tips. A black cap and gown hung over his arm, the uniform for the graduation ceremony. He was almost out the door when she stopped him.

"Dad, do you have a minute?"

He turned away from the front door. "I don't have long. Coach Chadwick is picking me up to

17

take me to the gym. I was going to wait for him on the porch. He'll be here any time."

She hung her head a little. "Oh. Well, I—"

"Hey, are you guys coming to the ceremony? I mean, you can use the car since I have a ride. Here, take the keys. I won't be needing—"

Mandy closed her eyes, bracing herself. "Dad, I don't want to be editor and chief of the *Crier* next year."

Her father froze with his arm extended. The car keys dangled from his fingers. An expression of concern and dismay replaced his cheerful demeanor.

Mandy had to keep going or she would never get it all out. "I know you bribed Mrs. Wilkins with ice-cream bars. I mean, she is the faculty sponsor for the *Crier*."

He made a funny face, as if he was trying to hide his disappointment. "Guilty as charged," he said. "Twelve cases of Pigeon Bars. I think she developed diabetes and lactose intolerance."

"Please, Dad, I'm serious. I never said I wanted to be editor of the paper. I want to be a reporter and a photographer. It's what I enjoy, what I do best."

He saw the pearl of a tear flowing down her smooth cheek. "Hey, it's okay," he replied in a kind voice. "I mean, if that's what you want. It's not the end of the world, honey."

Mandy wiped the pearl from her face. "Really? You're not mad?"

He shook his head. "No. It's your call, honey,

your life. I wouldn't want you to have it any other way. If you're sure this is what you want—"

"I'm sure."

"Then it's okay with me. I'll talk to Mrs. Wilkins the first chance I get. Is that all right?"

"Oh, Daddy."

They embraced in a father-daughter hug. A car horn sounded outside. Mr. Roberts opened the front door to see Coach Chadwick's station wagon parked in the street. Someone else was getting out of the passenger's side to transfer to the backseat.

Mr. Roberts grinned. "Now *there's* someone who might like to see you."

She gazed toward the boy in the coat and tie. Brett.

Her father urged her out the door. "Come on, I'll bet he wants to talk to you. Go on."

Buoyed by the resolution of her problem, Mandy felt light-hearted and enthusiastic. She preceded her father down the front steps, hurrying toward Brett, who hesitated with one hand on top of the open car door. His handsome face broke into a summer smile.

"School's out," he said. "Wow, Mandy, that suit looks great on you."

Mandy blushed. She wanted to kiss him suddenly, something that had not yet happened between them. She could not express her affections in front of her father and Coach Chadwick. Their first kiss would have to wait.

"Hi," she replied softly. "You're all dressed up."

Brett wore a striped swim-team tie, a blue

blazer, and khaki chinos. His penny loafers were freshly shined, his blond hair had been trimmed shorter. Tara was right, Mandy thought. Brett was a hunk.

"Sorry I missed your party," he said in a concerned tone. "All the members of the swim team have to act as ushers for graduation."

"It's okay," Mandy told him. "I did miss you, though."

His face looked hopeful. "Can we get together later, after the ceremony? There's going to be a lot of graduation parties."

Mandy touched his hand. "Sure. I might even see you at the graduation ceremony. Dad gave me the car."

"Cool. I—"

"Get in the car, Holloway! We haven't got all day!"

Coach Ralph Chadwick had bellowed the command from the driver's side of the station wagon. The burly, quarrelsome teacher was the same age as her father, but Chadwick was already bald and pot-bellied. He had a gruff, bearish disposition and a rough-looking exterior, but Mandy knew that her father's best friend was really a teddy bear on the inside. She found him harmless and lovable, a family friend for as long as she could remember.

She bent down, looking into the car with a wry grin. "Hi, Coach. How are you today?"

Coach Chadwick's round, chubby face barely approached a smile. "Oh, hi, Mandy. How are you?

Say hi to your mom for me. Gotta go. Come on, boys, load 'em up. We're out of here."

Her father sat down on the passenger's side. Brett got in and closed the back door. He was still looking at Mandy. She smiled and winked, telling them to drive safely.

Coach Chadwick grimaced. "Very funny, Mandy. I'm only the driver's ed instructor. I taught you how to drive!"

"I know," Mandy quipped. "You taught me all of your bad habits. That's why Dad never lets me borrow the car."

Coach Chadwick seemed to enjoy the good-natured kidding. "Mandy Roberts, you better thank your lucky stars that you aren't in any of my classes this year. I'd flunk you good!"

"No chance," she replied. "I have connections at Central. My dad is a counsellor there."

The coach pointed a finger at Brett. "I guess I'll have to take it out on your boyfriend here."

"Hey!" Brett said indignantly. "Come on, Coach."

Mandy ignored Coach Chadwick, giving her father a pat on the shoulder. "Don't let him drive too fast."

Vernon Roberts looked up at her, smiling. "See you later, Mando. Hey, I love you, kid."

She glanced back at Brett and rolled her eyes. "Later."

"After the ceremony," he replied. "We—"

Coach Chadwick cut short their farewell by putting the car into gear and roaring away down

Maplewood Drive, heading for the front gates of Prescott Estates. Mandy started to turn back to the house, but something drew her gaze to the departing vehicle. She watched for a moment, remembering what her father had said. *"I love you, kid."*

Why had he said it like that? He had never called her "kid" before. His face had appeared to be so serene and happy.

A shiver played through Mandy's bare shoulders. Clouds rolled over Port City to block the sun. The summer had abruptly grown cold. Mandy hurried inside to change into something warmer.

The clouds passed quickly, leaving the sun to awaken Port City. All of Mandy's neighbors were busy on Maplewood Drive, tending their lawns, putting in flowers. Red, yellow, purple, and white, the petunias, snapdragons, and pansies were the true stars of summer. Some of the gardeners waved to Mandy as she steered her father's Toyota Corolla toward Middle Street. Mandy gave them a short blast of a squeaky horn, prompting laughter from Steve and Tara.

"That horn is lame," Tara said.

Steve, who was stretched out in the backseat, gazed out the open window. "Why'd we leave so early anyway? The ceremony isn't for another hour. And we're only a few minutes from the school."

Mandy shrugged. "Uh, I thought we'd cruise,

see if we can find out where the good graduation parties are going to be."

"Cool," Steve replied.

They had changed clothes at Mandy's place. Steve wore a blue shirt and grey dress pants. Tara had on a flowery summer dress. Mandy chose a crimson skirt and a white blouse, the school colors for Central. It was the same outfit she had worn on her last date with Brett.

"Where are we cruising?" Tara asked.

Mandy cast a sideways look at her best friend. "Uh, I'm not sure yet."

Tara immediately understood Mandy's glance. She wanted to get rid of Steve, but she didn't want to hurt his feelings in the process. Tara figured Mandy wanted to talk about something personal and important. And they had to be alone.

Tara turned straight ahead, smiling. "Let's go through town. We can see what's happening."

Mandy turned onto Middle Street, passing Tremont Mall, following the run of the Tide Gate River until the street wound in toward town. She wanted to end up at the public library, where there might be something to distract Steve's attention. She was dying for a heart-to-heart with Tara, who was a great sounding board.

A detour at the corner of Bow Street took them left into the heart of Port City. Mandy turned right on Market Square Road, coasting slowly past the quaint brick buildings and colorful storefronts. The sidewalks were packed with shoppers and tourists. The summer season had started early for everyone, much to the delight of the town merchants.

Steve grinned at the crowd. "Cool. Port City is hopping. My dad says I can bus tables at the restaurant this summer if business picks up. Looks like it's going to be a busy vacation."

Mandy sighed. "I hope so."

Tara gave her an expectant look. "What?" she muttered.

Mandy nodded back toward Steve and moved her lips to say, "Later."

Steve didn't seem to catch on. Tara fidgeted in the passenger seat. She hated being left out of any gossipy secret.

They rolled through Market Square, merging onto Congress Street. Two rows of well-kept store-fronts graced Port City's main thoroughfare, where John Paul Jones and George Washington had once strode through the storybook little hamlet of the seacoast. They passed North Church and the Old Courthouse, crossing Middle Street again to complete the semicircle. Mandy turned into the parking lot of the public library, which had closed early because of Central's graduation day.

"Why are we stopping here?" Steve asked warily.

Mandy hoped he couldn't see it coming. "I thought we might find somebody here who would know about a good party." She gazed toward a group of four boys who were skateboarding and rollerblading in the deserted parking lot.

Tara made a face. "Those skate nerds?"

Mandy shot her a cautious look. "Tara! Those are Steve's *buds*!"

Steve sat up, peering over the back of the seat at the boys. "Hey, I know those dudes."

Tara nodded knowingly. "Oh, yeah."

Mandy parked close to the skaters so Steve could watch them. Steve loved rollerblading. Mandy was counting on that to be free of him.

"Hey," Steve said suddenly, "mind if I go hang with those guys?"

Mandy played it cool. "You said you were coming to the ceremony with us."

Steve moaned guilty. "Aw, I know. I guess I should stay with you then."

"Oh, go on," Mandy told him. "We'll call you tomorrow."

"All right!" Steve cried. "I'm out of here."

He bolted from the backseat, slamming the door behind him. His spidery legs jogged him toward the others. They met and slapped high-fives all around.

Mandy put the car into gear. "Mission accomplished."

"Smart move, Mando."

They emerged from the parking lot, turning back onto Middle Street. Restored Colonial-style houses lined the avenue. Some of the places were over two hundred years old. They wore the date of their building in dark numbers above the doorways.

"So what is it?" Tara demanded immediately.

Mandy grinned. "Brett."

Tara put her hands on her cheeks. "Nooo!"

"He was in the car with Coach Chadwick. He had on a tie and a blazer. He's so cute I can't stand it!"

"Mandy! You're the luckiest woman alive!"

Mandy took a deep breath, beaming with elation. "He's ushering today at the ceremony. I said I might see him there."

"Get going!" Tara insisted. "Don't let the speed limit stand in the way of true love!"

Mandy was light on the accelerator. "We'll be there in a minute. My dad trusted me with the car. I'm not going to get a ticket."

Tara turned toward her, gesturing with her hands. "Okay, I want to know—you don't have to tell me if you don't want to. But I'm dying to ask."

"What?"

"Is Brett a good kisser?"

Mandy grimaced with embarrassment. "Uh, I don't know—"

An expression of disbelief came to Tara's face. "What?"

"I know, I know. It just hasn't happened. But I know it will. I want it to happen. I do."

Tara rolled her eyes. "Kiss him."

"I will."

"I kissed Billy on our second date," Tara boasted.

"Brett isn't Billy," Mandy replied.

Tara raised a finger in the air. "True!"

Mandy sighed again. "I want a real relationship, Tara. I want to care about a guy because I know him, not just because he looks good."

Tara's smooth face grew serious. "That's real mature, Mandy. And I can see your point."

"I want to go steady for all the right reasons," Mandy went on. "Not because I can have the cutest boy in school."

Tara shrugged. "Yeah, but I'm willing to give the cute boys a chance at the front of the line. You know what I'm saying?"

Mandy laughed so hard that she had to pull over. Tara was also giggling and acting bonkers. They were giddy, happy beyond belief. Nothing could spoil the summer vacation for them.

Or so they thought.

THREE

Port City was lucky to have a high school like Central Academy. The campus was made up of three classroom buildings of red brick, as well as a combination gymnasium/auditorium, a great library, an indoor swimming pool, a football/soccer stadium, and several baseball diamonds. The academy had been built while Mandy and Tara were still in middle school. From the start, the faculty and administration had adopted a policy of stressing academics which put many students, Mandy and Tara included, into college prep classes during the last year of study.

By the time Mandy and Tara arrived at Central, the faculty parking lot and the student parking lot were both half full. Mandy drove past the other cars, cruising along the far side of the gymnasium. No one had parked in back of the gym. Mandy guided the Toyota to a halt under a fire escape that rose to the high roof of the building.

Tara frowned. "What are you doing?"

"Parking the car."

"We'll have to walk all the way around to go in to the ceremony!"

Mandy opened her door. "No, we won't."

Tara got out with her. "Mandy—"

Mandy walked around behind the car, taking a step up on the rear bumper. With Tara watching skeptically, Mandy pulled down the iron ladder that led to the fire stairs. She braced herself for the climb.

Tara shook her head. "You're going to get your blouse dirty. What do you think you're doing anyway?"

Mandy ignored her, scaling the ladder to a platform at the base of the iron steps. The flight of stairs led to one high door above them. Tara had to wonder where the door would take them. She was sure that Mandy had gone nuts on her.

"Where are you going?" Tara asked again.

"I'm not going to tell you. If you want to come, you'll have to follow me."

"Oh, all right. Wait for me."

Tara climbed to the platform, grumbling all the way. "You've lost it, Mandy. I mean it."

"You'll love it," Mandy replied. "You'll be able to see everything. Dad showed me last year."

They started slowly upward, taking each step carefully on the rickety fire escape, their hands clamped tightly on the railing.

Tara wanted to talk, to keep her mind off the

height. "Hey, did you ever tell your dad about the *Crier?*"

Mandy nodded. "It's all settled. I think he's going to take another box of ice-cream bars to Mrs. Wilkins to get me out of it."

"Your dad is the greatest, Mandy."

"I know."

When they reached the last iron step, Tara saw the door up close. "What if it's locked?"

"The janitor has to open all fire doors the day of an event," Mandy replied. "Dad told me."

Mandy turned the knob and pushed open the door. A rush of cool air flowed from the gym. Mandy stepped through the doorway, followed by Tara. They emerged on a steel mesh catwalk that ran all the way back into the shady rafters of the roof. Mandy and Tara could see everything below them from the high perch.

"Wow," Tara said, "you were right. It really is worth it."

Mandy peered at the graduation festivities in the making. "They film the basketball games from up here. Hey, there's Dad."

Vernon Roberts walked across the stage floor, pulling a long, black cord from beneath the bleachers that had been erected for the Central faculty members. He drew the wire close to a speaker's podium. Mandy remembered that it was his job to work the public address system. As usual, her devoted dad was in the middle of everything, trying his best to do a good job.

"Oh, Mandy, it's gorgeous."

Mandy's eyes followed the red and white streamers that festooned the entire gym with Central's colors. Outside, seniors were gathering in alphabetical order, over three hundred of them, ready to begin the march down the aisle of folding chairs that formed a row on the gym floor. Coach Chadwick's gruff voice rose in the building as he barked orders to the members of the swim team who ushered in the spectators. Mandy looked hopefully for Brett but she didn't see him.

The bleachers were filling steadily with parents and friends of the graduating seniors. Back on stage, her father had left the microphone to test the sound system that was to play the ceremonial music. Teachers and administrators filed past Vernon Roberts to crowd the faculty bleachers directly behind the podium. A table had been stacked high with phony, red-ribboned scrolls to serve as diplomas. The real certificates would arrive in the mail later to avoid confusion.

"It's perfect," Mandy said.

The first strains of *Pomp and Circumstance* reverberated through the PA system, blaring into the rafters for a moment. The music stopped when her father reset the tape. All the pieces were in place. Mandy hoped her own graduation was this impeccable.

Tara sighed. "It's all so neat."

"Neat, huh!"

Mandy and Tara snapped to attention. The raspy male voice had come out of the rafters. Something dropped from the shadows, landing with a thud. The catwalk trembled under the force of the heavier body. A dark figure started to move toward them.

Tara grabbed Mandy's arm. "Let's get out of here."

Mandy wheeled bravely to face the intruder. "Who's there? Why are you hiding from us?"

A rough-looking, pimply-faced boy slid into the dim light. His dirty red hair had been slicked back and shaved punk-style on the sides. He wore stiff jeans and a leather jacket. Thick boot soles clomped on the iron mesh.

"Nobody says neat anymore, sweetheart," he told Tara.

Mandy knew him immediately—Jimmy "the Deuce" Boatman. His narrow eyes gave her the head-to-toe once-over. Mandy was afraid, but she wasn't about to let Jimmy know it.

"What are you doing up here?" she asked firmly.

Jimmy took a crumpled pack of Camels from a leather pocket and stuffed an unfiltered cigarette between his thin lips. "I'm bein' neat, sweet thing. Neat. Who says neat but the little teenage queen and her friend, Mandy Roberts? Sugar wouldn't melt on Miss Port City."

Mandy suddenly felt feverish. "There's no smoking in the gym."

Jimmy chortled, struck a match, torched the cigarette, and then held the match in front of his eyes. "What if I burned down the whole freakin' place? Huh? Poof, ashes. No diplomas, no graduation. I could spoil the day for all those snooty brats."

Tara leaned close to Mandy, whispering in a tenative voice. "How'd this pyscho get into Central?"

Mandy replied from the corner of her mouth, "He's one of my father's charity cases. It's the only school he hasn't been asked to leave yet."

Jimmy snuffed out the match and threw it over the edge. Smoke circled around his face as he eased toward them. Tara backed away, hiding behind Mandy.

"Don't be afraid, honey," Jimmy said through the cloud of haze, "I'm okay. I'm one of you, thanks to your old man, Roberts. I've got a solid *C* average. I'm going to graduate next year with all of you Prescott pukes."

"We better go, Tara," Mandy said calmly. "Dad will be—"

Before they could even turn away, Jimmy darted past them, standing between the girls and the door. "How's your old man, Mandy? Is he still a bleedin' heart? Gonna save all us delinquents?"

"We have to go, Jimmy," Mandy insisted.

Jimmy reached out, grabbing both rails of the catwalk. "Your old man is a sucker, Roberts. A dweeb, a geek, a wuss. You know?"

Mandy scowled at him. "Get out of the way, Jimmy. Or—"

"Or what? You gonna tell your dah-dah? Mr. All-American. You gonna get me expelled?"

Her father had told her about Jimmy Boatman.

He had come from an abusive home, after which he had bounced from school to school, from foster home to foster home. Being admitted to Central was Jimmy's last chance. Everyone had been waiting for him to blow it. He was getting close.

"Oh, we're going to be on the six o'clock news," Tara said. "I wonder if they'll show the carnage of our decaying bodies."

Mandy kept her eyes on Jimmy's hands. "It's probably best not to rile him. There's not going to be any trouble, is there, Jimmy? You're going to let us leave, aren't you?"

His laugh was nasty, full of insinuations. Something clicked in his right hand. Mandy saw the flash of a steel blade. She backpedaled, taking Tara with her for a few steps. Holding the blade in front of him, Jimmy began to advance like a predator.

"What's wrong?" he asked mockingly. "There's not going to be any trouble, is there, Miss Cream Cheese? I'm just going to clean my fingernails with this pigsticker. Hey, are your fingernails dirty?"

Mandy matched her retreat to his movement. "This isn't funny, Jimmy. Stop it now and I won't tell anyone what you did."

Jimmy stopped, tapping the palm of his hand with the flat of the blade. "Nobody rides for free, Mandy. Tell you what. If you'll go out with me—tonight—I'll let you walk away. How's that sound?"

"You're out of your mind," Mandy replied with a nervous laugh.

Tara winced behind her. "Great, Mandy. Now he has a reason to kill us. Before it was just for fun."

"One date, Miss Port City," Jimmy said, tossing the knife back and forth between his hands. "One date or I'll—wha—hey—"

Jimmy's body buckled. His head flew backward. The knife dropped on the catwalk at Mandy's feet. She grabbed the handle and held the weapon in front of her.

Suddenly Jimmy fell forward, landing facedown on the shaking catwalk. Brett Holloway put a knee to the boy's back, pinning him. Now Jimmy was the helpless one.

"Get him!" Tara said.

Brett twisted Jimmy's arm behind his back and then glanced up at Mandy. "Lose the knife."

Mandy folded the blade and dropped the weapon into the empty bleachers below them. "Brett, how did you—"

"Your father saw his car go through the parking lot," Brett replied quickly. "When you didn't show up right away, he sent me to look for you. I found the car downstairs. I figured you came up here. I know about this place because I helped to film a couple of the home games."

"Big freakin' deal," Jimmy grunted. "Now get off me, jock boy."

Brett turned his arm again to make him wince

with pain. "All right, I'm going to let you up. But you better chill."

Releasing his knee from Jimmy's back, Brett stood up straight. Jimmy scrambled to his feet, immediately swinging hard at Brett, who easily avoided the blow. Jimmy lost his balance, falling into the rail of the catwalk. He would have gone over the edge if Brett hadn't grabbed him and pulled him back onto the mesh platform. Jimmy regained his balance, clutching the rail.

Brett moved over in front of Mandy and Tara. "Time for you to split, Deuce. The party's finished."

Jimmy pointed a finger at them. "You preps, you're all dog meat. You hear me? When I get through with you, the only thing you will be good for is a dirt nap."

Brett's arms hung loosely by his sides. "I'm quaking."

Tara peeked around him. "Yeah, Deuce, we're quaking."

Mandy tugged her back. "Tara!"

Jimmy turned and fled, slamming the door behind him.

Brett spun to face Mandy. "Are you all right?" he said gently.

She nodded. Her hands were trembling. She had to grip the rail to keep them from seeing how scared she had been. Why did a guy like Jimmy always have to spoil the happiness of others?

Tara put her hands on her hips. "He'd better get

out of here. I was just ready to scratch his face off!"

Mandy and Brett did not hear her. They were standing together, their eyes locked. Something wonderful was taking place.

Brett held one of Mandy's hands. "I'm going to tell your father about that creep. He's history around here."

Mandy touched his cheek. "No! I mean, not today. Forget about it. He wasn't really going to hurt us. He just wanted to freak us out."

Brett was actually blushing like a bashful sophomore. "Are you sure?"

She took his arm. "Yes. I'd rather be happy today. Wouldn't you?"

He nodded and took a deep breath. "I guess. I just can't stand the idea of the jerk bothering you."

Mandy smiled. "He's gone. We're here."

Tara suddenly realized what had happened right in front of her own eyes. Mandy and Brett were finally connecting. He had saved her from the evil clutches of the Deuce. She stepped back, closing her mouth, watching them go on like she wasn't even there.

Brett reached into the pocket of his blazer. "Hey, check this out. I mean, here, I have something I want you to see." He put something cool and metallic into Mandy's hand.

She held the chunk of gold up to her eyes. "Your class ring. It's great. When did you get it? Mine's still on order."

"I got it today," Brett replied. "I haven't even worn it yet. I—I was wondering if you would—well—"

Mandy's heart was looking for an escape route from her throbbing chest. "Yes, Brett?"

Tara bit her finger. "He's going to do it," she muttered.

Brett laughed and sighed. "I wanted to be so cool when I did this. I—well, we're seniors now, so I—I mean, we can wear our rings. You can wear mine. I mean, if you want to."

"Okay."

Brett's face lit up. "You mean it?"

Mandy nodded.

Brett threw out his hands. "That's it. We're going steady."

"Well, Holloway, go ahead and kiss her!"

The voice of Mandy's prankster father echoed through the rafters of the gym. Mandy wheeled toward the stage. Vernon Roberts had been watching from behind the microphone. A spotlight swung around to bathe the happy couple in a wash of bright radiance. All eyes lifted to gawk at them.

Brett grabbed Mandy's hand. "Come on, I'll take you backstage."

A red-faced Mandy followed him, all the time glaring at the man in the black cap and gown who stood at the podium. She couldn't see his face, but she knew he was laughing. Everyone thought it was funny but Mandy!

"I'm going to get him!" Mandy said under her breath.

Tara found it impossible not to smile. "Oh, lighten up. He's right. It's about time you and Brett kissed each other."

Mandy shook her fist at the stage. "When I get through with him, he's going to be one dead dad!"

FOUR

As soon as Mandy, Brett, and Tara arrived at the backstage area, Coach Chadwick began to bellow. "Where have you been, Holloway? You're supposed to be an usher. Now get out there and *ush*!"

Brett rolled his eyes at Mandy before he fled to his duties. He followed a narrow passageway between the bleachers and the wings. The faculty seats covered almost all of the stage. Brett disappeared into the ever-growing graduation crowd.

Mandy clutched the ring in her right hand. It had been a strange day, up and down. But everything had come out okay in the end.

Tara gazed at the imposing structure of the bleachers. "Wow, there must be twenty rows."

Coach Chadwick appeared beside them. "Big faculty, needed a lot of seats. Hey, you kids want a ringside seat at the ceremony?"

Mandy nodded, half in a love trance. "Sure, Coach."

"I'm sure not sitting on those bleachers," Tara said.

Coach Chadwick waved and turned downstage, taking the same path that Brett had followed. Mandy and Tara lagged behind him, trailing the coach in the shade of the bleachers. Above their heads, the wooden tiers squeaked and rattled as the teachers searched for seat assignments.

"Looks like a *Star Trek* convention," Tara quipped. "Why are the faculty wearing black? The students are wearing red gowns."

"Another tradition my father started," Mandy replied.

The hum of voices buzzed in the air like dull music. Mandy could feel the electricity, the excitement of the impending ceremony. And Brett's ring made everything more intense. She had never been this happy before.

Coach Chadwick ducked in behind a line of curtains. Mandy and Tara stopped. Where was he going? His face loomed back at them from the curtain. He waved for the girls to follow.

Mandy and Tara eased behind the heavy gray curtain. They inched their way down a musty corridor between the curtain and the wall, finally emerging in the bright reflection of the overhead stage lights. There were two director's chairs sitting in the wings.

Coach Chadwick gestured to the empty seats. "Your father and I were going to sit here, but we won't get a chance. Mandy, you and your little friend can take these chairs."

Tara immediately plopped into the red and white chair. "We're stars, Mando. Big time."

Mandy sat down with the ring still heavy in her hand. "Thank you, Uncle Ralph."

Coach Chadwick grimaced like an angry bear. "Uncle Ralph! It's been ten years since you called me that."

"She's in love," Tara quipped.

"Hush!" Mandy told her.

Coach Chadwick's face turned red. "Well, gotta go. Keep things running behind the scenes. Your father and me are busy today. Say hi to your mom for me, Mandy. Is she here?"

Mandy shook her head. "I don't think so. She finds this stuff boring."

"So do I," Coach Chadwick replied. "See you later, girls."

He hurried off to tend to some backstage necessity.

Tara frowned after him. "I think he's drinking too much coffee. He never slows down."

Mandy's green eyes had begun to search the aisles for Brett. People were still filing in steadily. The gym was almost full. She looked hard but she couldn't find her new steady.

The graduates would be marching soon, but all that Mandy could think about was Brett's class ring, now in her possession. Was this how it felt to have a dream come true? She was practically floating in midair.

Tara turned quickly with an expectant glint in

her dark eyes. "Okay, let's see the ring. Live and in color."

Mandy slowly unfolded her hand, like she was holding a tiny bird that might escape her grasp. The Central class ring caught the spill of the stage lights. Tara eyed it closely, never daring to actually touch the prize.

"I bet he had it made at Goldman's Jewelry," Tara said. "It's better than the ones we ordered."

Mandy closed her hand again. "I never realized how I felt until I saw him up there." She pointed to the catwalk in the rafters.

Tara shook her head. "Boatman. What a creep. I'm going to tell your father the first chance I get."

The incident with the Deuce had seemed like a bad dream. In her present state of grace, Mandy couldn't think of anything but Brett. She told Tara to forget about Jimmy Boatman, at least for a couple of days.

Tara leaned back in the chair. "Wow, a steady for the summer. Brett's dad has a boat, too, out at Agony Bluff. Of course, you'll want me along for company. And I bet your new man has a couple of cute friends for me."

Mandy saw it all before her. A perfect summer and her senior class. She knew it was going to be the best year of her life.

"Attention. Test, one, two, three—"

She lifted her eyes to the stage. Her father was back at the microphone, doing a sound check. Mandy glared thunder and lightning at him, though she had to work harder at it since her temper had cooled. Since all had ended well, her father's prank did not seem to matter as much.

As Vernon Roberts turned away from the microphone, he caught Mandy's steely staring act from the wings. His mouth curled into a sly smile and he threw out his hands. Mandy tried to hold her scowling expression, but her father pointed a finger at her as if to say, "Gotcha." They ended up laughing at each other. He finally turned away and went to the other side of the stage to run the sound system for the graduation march.

"This is it," Tara said. "Look. It's old Vandy."

Principal Harriet Vandaway, a distinguished, white-haired woman, was ascending to the lectern. She stepped up to the microphone, shuffling her notes for a moment. Mrs. Vandaway was one of the most distinguished educators in the history of New England. Her genius had made Central come to life.

"Oh, I'm so glad we came," Tara whispered.

Mandy couldn't stop smiling. "Me, too."

Principal Vandaway gave a brief welcoming speech and then launched into several announcements. She acknowledged the faculty who sat behind her on the overflowing bleachers. Then she introduced an addition to the Central administration, the assistant principal for the coming year, Harlan Kinsley. A reed-slim, auburn-haired gentleman stood up, nodding to the crowd. Mandy and Tara paid little attention to him.

Mandy kept looking for Brett. She finally spotted him leaning against the front apron of the stage. Mandy watched him closely. Brett didn't seem to be doing much in the way of ushering. He was in the same trance that had taken hold of Mandy.

Suddenly, Brett looked up and peered straight at her, as if he had felt her gaze. His face beamed. They were connecting all the way across the gym. It was so right for the moment.

The sharp screeching of feedback blared over the PA system, startling Mandy back to the matters at hand. Music came behind the awful, intrusive noise. *Pomp and Circumstance* echoed through the lonely rafters of the building.

Central's graduating seniors had their cue. Clad in their red gowns and mortarboards, they entered the gym, marching in from three different doors. The procession moved slowly down the aisles.

"Cool," Tara said.

Mandy's emotions were soaring. "It's all so—so perfect."

As soon as the words had left her lips, the music died. A hush quieted the audience. Some of the graduates stopped in their tracks, not sure what to do. Red and white tassels swung back and forth as they looked around for someone to guide them.

"Drat!"

The voice of Vernon Roberts rose above the silence. Mandy saw him walking toward the principal. He told her to test the microphone. Principal Vandaway found that the mike wasn't working. Mandy's father grimaced and his eyes grew wide.

Tara bit her fingers. "Uh-oh, your dad is in trouble."

"On no!" Mandy said under her breath.

Vernon Roberts was now running straight toward his daughter, scuffling across the stage in the flowing robe. Just before he reached Mandy and Tara, he stopped, lifting one finger in the air to assure everyone that he would save the day once more. The crowd laughed and applauded.

Mandy grinned. "What a guy. He's handling it."

"Cool."

Her father flew by them, heading for the rear scaffolding of the faculty bleachers.

Mandy came off the chair and followed after him. "Dad."

Her nerves were tingling all through her body. Something did not feel right. She watched her father climb under the bleachers, disappearing into the dull light beneath the tiers.

"Dad!"

"I'll be all right," he called back. "Something just came loose. I think I know which wire it is."

His dark figure went deeper into the shadows. Above him, the bleachers were shaking as some of the faculty members tried to look down into the hollow of the structure.

"Here it is," he called in a confident voice.

A tremor played through the stage floor. Mandy sensed the vibrations on the soles of her shoes. Something was really wrong.

"Dad, get out of there. Dad!"

"No, Mandy, I got it. I—"

"Dad!"

Mr. Roberts began to scream at the top of his lungs. He begged for help as his body twitched with the power of a sudden electric jolt. Mandy could hear the sparking from the current. Thin smoke began to curl around her father's spasmodic form.

Mandy started to go in after him. But as soon as she touched the metal frame, another burst of current knocked her away. She landed on her backside five feet from the disaster.

The electricity flowed through the ironwork of the scaffold, sparking and smoking the faculty members. They panicked, scuffling to get off the death-trap structure. The bleachers started to sway back and forth under the shifting weight.

Scrambling to her feet, Mandy stood there helplessly listening to her father's painful cries. She had to save him. She took another step toward the quaking bleachers. A strong hand yanked her back.

Coach Chadwick grabbed her shoulder to restrain her. "Mandy, don't touch that thing. You'll be electrocuted."

"Help him!" Mandy cried.

Coach Chadwick shouted to the wings. "Hit the power! Kill the switch!"

There was too much commotion for anyone to hear him.

"Stay here," he told Mandy. "I'm gonna kill the power."

When he was gone, she wanted to move closer to the bleachers. "Dad!"

Tara stopped her. "Stay here, Mandy." Tara tried to pull her back, but Mandy did not want to go.

"Help him! Someone!"

A sharp, cracking sound started through the middle of the bleachers. The tiers all shifted inward. The trembling became a roar.

"It's falling!" Tara cried.

Mandy jumped away from the collapsing bleachers, pushing Tara out of harm's way. They escaped the fatal implosion. But the entire wreckage of the structure came crashing down on her father.

Staggering to her feet again, Mandy gazed with disbelieving eyes at the carnage. She screamed for someone to rescue her father. Why couldn't someone just help him?"

The lights went out. Mandy and Tara huddled for a moment in the darkness. There were screams and cries of pain all around them. Coach Chadwick appeared out of nowhere, guiding the terrified girls toward the emergency exit.

Mandy tried to look back, but the coach wouldn't let her. She kept screaming as she clung to her father's closest friend. The burly Chadwick dragged them safely through the emergency doorway.

There was nothing else for Mandy to do except

pray that her father had somehow survived the catastrophe.

Mandy sat in back of the ambulance between two wide-open doors. A blanket had been wrapped around her shoulders by one of the paramedics. The police and fire departments had also arrived to help restore order. All of them were inside the gym, no doubt, Mandy thought, saving her father from the hideous wreckage.

He had to survive. Mandy could not live without him. Someone's shadow fell unexpectedly at her feet.

She looked up. "Dad?"

Tara took a deep breath. "No, only me."

Mandy put her hands over her green eyes. The pain had to go away. She couldn't bear it much longer. Her father had to be all right.

"Here," Tara said blankly. "Drink this."

Mandy refused the paper cup of water. All the joy of the day had dissolved into grief and sorrow. She kept looking at the exit every few seconds, expecting her father to step out of the gym with a smile on his face. He would tell her that everything was going to be all right. Just a scratch here and there.

"Where is he?"

"Mandy?"

Barbara Roberts stood there behind the ambulance with her arms extended toward her daughter. Tears flowed down her face. Mandy ran to her, embracing. They cried for a long time before the policeman approached the ambulance.

Mandy could perceive the doleful expression on the young patrolman's face. Her green eyes flickered toward the exit door. Two men were bringing a stretcher from the smoky building. The body had been covered with a sheet.

Mrs. Roberts began to tremble violently. "Oh no. God, no!"

The young patrolman shook his head and looked sheepishly at the ground.

Mandy felt numb inside. She watched the stretcher going into a white van, which quickly moved away from curb after the doors were closed. Her mother collapsed suddenly, falling backward.

Mandy could not believe it.

Her father was really dead.

FIVE

Shadows surrounded Mandy in the confines of her dim bedroom. She could not escape the dark vision of her father's death. Every time she closed her eyes to try to sleep, the images stirred in her head, returning her to a cold, hostile world where nothing made any sense.

She kept torturing herself with the most devastating question: Why had it happened to her? How could someone like Vernon Roberts, a warm, kind, generous man, be taken from her in such a horrifying manner? One moment he had been there joking with her, then he was gone in an instant. There was no reason for his demise, none that Mandy could perceive.

Lying back with her head on the pillow, Mandy waited for the tears to come to her green eyes. But she could no longer cry. A dull, ever-present pain had replaced the tears. Heartache weighed on her soul with the pressure of a stone boulder. She would never be able to free herself of the agony.

How would she be able to live without her father? Nothing could fill the emptiness that had taken over her life. She had fallen into a deep, bottomless hole and she would never be able to climb out of it. All of Mandy's hopes had been lowered into the ground with her father's coffin.

The funeral had been a continuation of the unbelievable nightmare. Rain fell on the procession. Even in the bad weather, a large crowd turned out to pay their last respects. Most of the faculty and half the student body attended the graveside service. But the show of love and support had been little comfort for Mandy. Nothing would bring her father back.

A heated rush of anger seized her. She wanted to fight somebody, to hurt someone the way she had been hurt. There had to be a way to battle back, to take revenge. But how could she fight death? What good was her rage if there was no place to vent it? She would have cursed the hateful turns of fate, but her father had taught her not to swear.

She finally managed to close her eyes. She slept for a while, but the dream came again, the way it had come every day since the funeral.

Her father was standing poolside in their back-yard. He was smiling, waving to her. Mandy tried to run to him but she could not move. Her arms and legs were frozen. If she could only reach him, she could warn him not to go to the graduation ceremony. He was alive again and she had to tell him to stay away from the gym at Central.

Mandy cried out and sat up in her bed. Sweat

poured off her face. Her body was weak. She hated the dream. She hated everything since her father had died.

A light knocking resounded from her bedroom door. "Mandy? Are you all right?"

Her mother was at the door. She had come upstairs to check on her. Mandy really didn't want to talk to anyone, not even her mother.

"Mandy. Please answer me."

Mandy fell back on the pillows. "Go away, Mom."

"Let me come in, honey. Just for a minute. Please."

Mandy ignored her, hoping she would leave.

"Honey, please. Just for a minute. Can I come in?"

"I don't care," Mandy muttered under her breath.

"Honey?"

"I don't care!" Mandy snapped.

The door to Mandy's room creaked open slowly. Light spilled in from the second-story hallway. Mrs. Roberts entered, reeking of cigarettes and whiskey. Her hair was a mess, her clothes rumpled. She wasn't faring any better than her daughter in the aftermath of losing her husband.

"Hi," she said softly. "I just came up to see how you were."

"I'm okay, Mom. You don't have to worry about me."

"I'm not so sure about that."

Mrs. Roberts eased through the shadows, flipping on an overhead light. Mandy flinched at the brightness, covering her eyes with the back of her hand. She resented the light. Her father had been a shining beacon, but he had been snuffed out like a candle in a hurricane.

"Turn it off," she told her mother.

Mrs. Roberts switched off the light and sat on the edge of Mandy's bed. "Mandy, you can't stay in here forever."

"Why not?" Mandy scoffed. "There's nothing outside for me. I'm happy in here. Leave me alone. I'll be fine."

"Honey—"

Mrs. Roberts tried to take her hand, but Mandy pulled away. No one could console her, not even her other living parent. They had gotten along together all of Mandy's life, but since the funeral, they were like strangers. Her father had always been the glue that held the family together. After his death, the chasm between them had opened up, and there didn't seem to be any way to bridge it.

Mrs. Roberts sighed. "Mandy, it's been two weeks since the funeral. You can't stay in here forever. Your friends have been calling."

"So?"

"Honey, I know you're sad and angry. But you can't withdraw. You have to face it head on. Isn't that what your father taught you?"

Mandy just ignored her, staring into space. It didn't matter what her father would have wanted. He was dead now.

"Steve and Tara are worried sick about you," Mrs. Roberts went on. "And Brett has been calling."

Brett. Mandy hadn't thought about him very much lately. His ring was on her vanity table, sitting in her jewelry box. Technically, they were still going steady, though that fact meant nothing to her. She no longer wondered about the sweetness of the first kiss that had never come.

"Why don't you call Tara, honey? Go to the beach or something."

Mandy's green eyes remained focused on the blank whiteness of the ceiling. "Go to the beach? Oh, that's rich, Mom. The beach. That'll make everything better. For sure."

The tone of her mother's voice hardened a little. "He's gone, Mandy. We both have to accept it. Your father would want us to go on with our lives. We have to keep on living without him."

"He can't want anything," Mandy replied. "He's dead!"

"Mandy—"

"Leave me alone, Mom."

"You aren't the only one with feelings," Mrs. Roberts told her. "I miss him, too. But it's been two weeks and you haven't come out of this room. I'm worried about you, baby."

"I'm not your baby anymore."

For a moment, Mrs. Roberts looked as if she was about to cry. But she had also run out of tears. Mandy knew she should reach out to her mother, but something stopped her. She could only feel anger and resentment for everything in her life, even the woman who sat on the edge of her bed trying to comfort her. It was impossible for Mandy to feel love. The emotion had died when her father was taken from her.

"Mandy, this can't go on," her mother said sadly. "We've got to—"

"Can't you just leave me alone, Mom?"

"Why don't you eat something, honey? I know, we could order a pizza."

Mandy's eyes narrowed and focused on her mother. "Pizza?"

"You have to eat, Mandy."

"What about you?" Mandy scoffed. "Do you have to eat? Or do you just have to numb yourself?"

"Mandy, please—"

"You have a lot of nerve to lecture me," Mandy went on in a vicious tone. "You sit downstairs in front of the television, smoking your cigarettes and drinking your cheap whiskey!"

"That's not fair, Mandy!"

"Oh sure! It's okay for you to be sad, but I can't be unhappy. Is that fair? Huh? Tell me, Mommy. Is that fair?"

Her mother tensed and stood up. Resentment was evident in her face. She turned away from Mandy.

"Just leave me alone!" Mandy cried again.

Mrs. Roberts glared at her. "You're not the only one who lost him. I lost him, too. Do you hear me?"

Mandy looked away. "I don't hear anything."

Mrs. Roberts sighed. "You'd better get yourself together. We're having company tonight."

"What?"

"Company," her mother replied. "Guests."

Mandy frowned at the ceiling. "I don't want any company. Tell them not to come."

Mrs. Roberts fumbled with a pack of cigarettes, putting one into her mouth. "This isn't the kind of company you can turn away. The chief of police is coming over. He wants to ask us some questions about—about the accident. He wants to talk to you, too."

"What if I don't want to talk to him?" Mandy snipped.

"You don't have any choice," her mother replied coldly. "They're coming at seven."

"They?"

"Coach Chadwick will be here, too. So will Steve and Tara. You'd better be ready. I don't want any of this attitude when they arrive. They're guests in our home. We'll treat them as such."

Mrs. Roberts turned away, leaving Mandy's room, closing the door behind her.

Mandy just lay there in the shadows. She felt awful about the way they had been fighting since the funeral. She knew she should be more supportive. She wanted to be kind to her mother, but somehow she couldn't do it.

The darkness was so strong in Mandy's heart that she wondered if she would ever know the light again.

The summer day was bright again, warm and inviting in the backyard at the Roberts house. Mandy gazed across the pool toward the barbecue grill. Her father stood there in his silly costume, turning the burgers, smiling at her in his special way. He was alive. The accident had never hap-

*pened. Mandy could tell him not to go to the gym.
Everything would be all right again.*

"Dad! Hey, Daddy!"

Vernon Roberts waved back to her, grinning.

"Dad, you can't go to the gym today. Do you hear
me? You have to stay away from school."

He did not seem to hear her.

She had to make him understand. "Dad, the
bleachers will fall in on you. You can't go to Central.
You have to stay here with me, Dad. Please."

*He kept on turning the burgers as if nothing
would go wrong. He seemed oblivious to her warn-
ings. She had to get him to listen.*

"Dad!"

*She tried to move toward him but her feet were
frozen to the concrete surface around the edges of
the pool. Her arms and legs were useless. There
had to be a way to get to him.*

"Dad, please!"

*She had to warn him while he was still alive. If
she could just stop him from going to the graduation ceremony—but she was fixed like a statue in
Fair Common Park. She squirmed, trying to free
herself.*

"Dad!"

"Mandy."

The image of her father faded before her.
Mandy opened her eyes. There was another figure
hovering in front of her. Strong hands rested on
her shoulders.

"Dad?" she asked with hope in her voice.

She sat up quickly, expecting her father to be there.

"Dad, it's you!"

"No, Mandy, it's me, Brett." He sat on the edge of her bed. "Hi."

Her face went slack. "Brett? How did you—"

"Your mother said I could come up to see you," he replied in a soft voice. "I just wanted to—"

Mandy removed his hands from her shoulders. "No. Get away. Leave me alone."

Brett stood, taking a couple of steps backward. "Hey, I'm sorry. I—I didn't mean to upset you."

Mandy threw her legs over the side of the bed, wiping her eyes. The dream had seemed so real. Her father had been alive again for a few moments. Was the nightmare going to haunt her forever?

"You mom said you were sleeping all day," Brett offered.

Mandy glared at him. "Why did you come here?"

A hurt expression spread over his handsome face. "I—I wanted to see you. You haven't returned any of my calls."

"So?"

"I'm worried about you, Mandy. It's been two weeks. You haven't spoken to any of your friends. We're all worried."

"Don't be," she replied. "I don't need any of you to worry about me. Now get out of my room."

"Mandy, I thought we were going steady. I care about you. I want to help any way I can."

She sighed impatiently. "Forget it, Brett. I don't need this. Just go, all right?"

He took a step toward her, reaching out. "Mandy, please."

Jumping off the bed, Mandy brushed past him, heading for her vanity. Her fingers fumbled with the lid of her jewelry box. Even in the shadows, Brett's ring still shone from the box. She took it out and thrust it toward him.

Brett was deeply wounded by the thoughtless gesture. "No, Mandy. Not like this. Please."

"Just take it," she said blankly. "I don't want it."

"But I thought—"

"Don't think, Brett. We aren't going steady anymore."

"Don't do this, Mandy."

"Take it!"

He plucked the ring from her outstretched hand. "I'm sorry, Mandy. It doesn't have to be this way."

She pointed toward the door. "Get out, Brett. And don't come back."

He hung his head. "I can't leave just yet. I have to stay for a little while. The chief of police wants me here tonight. He's going to talk to all of us about—about what happened."

Mandy touched her palm to her forehead. She didn't want to talk to anyone about the accident. She just wanted to be left alone.

Brett came closer, trying to take her hand. "Mandy—"

She grimaced, slapping at him. "I told you to get off me."

Brett was on the verge of tears. "Mandy, please

tell me why you're treating me like this. I thought we had something special."

"We don't."

"I want to be there for you, Mandy."

"I told you to get out!"

Brett turned slowly toward the door. "It doesn't have to be this way. We can all help you."

"Can't you move any faster!" Mandy cried.

Tears had begun to roll down his face. He started for the hall, stopping once to gaze back at her before he left. But Mandy would not look into his eyes.

"I'm sorry," he said softly as he closed the door.

Mandy ignored his hurt puppy-dog expression. She didn't want him to help her. She didn't need help from anyone.

Stepping to her bedroom window, she pulled back the curtain and peered down at the street. A police car was parked in the eerie light of dusk that had begun to spread over Port City. Steve and Tara were just arriving in a car that belonged to Tara's father. They got out and started up the front walk.

Mandy closed the curtain. She did not want to talk to anyone, not even her friends. What good would it do to talk to anyone? They couldn't help her. They couldn't bring her father back.

She heard her mother calling from the living room. Mandy took a deep breath. Like it or not, she had to go down and face them.

SIX

Mandy slogged reluctantly down the staircase, scuffling her bare feet on the thick carpet. Clad in a rumpled white T-shirt and faded jeans, she looked like an unmade bed. Her messy hair sprawled in a hundred different directions, covering half her face.

When she entered the living room, her mother, drink and cigarette in hand, frowned her disapproval. "So glad you could dress up for us."

Mandy ignored her, dropping limply into an easy chair. She gazed at the floor and folded her arms over her torso. She didn't care what they thought of her. They hadn't lost their fathers.

"Sit up straight, dear," her mother intoned. "Chief Danridge would like to ask you a few questions."

Victor Danridge, Chief of the Port City Police Department, sat on the sofa next to Barbara Roberts. He was a young, handsome man with penetrating blue eyes. Instead of a uniform, Chief

Danridge wore a dark business suit. He had been a lawyer before taking the job in Port City. Mandy's father had commented that the town was lucky to have Vic Danridge on the job.

Coach Chadwick was also on the sofa, sitting to the left of Mandy's mother. He seemed grim and thoughtful. He kept glancing over at Mandy, but she would not acknowledge him.

Nor would she look at Steve, Tara, or Brett, who sat on folding chairs on the other side of the living room. Steve bit his nails, unsure as to why he had been called to this meeting. Tara tried to get Mandy's attention, unsuccessfully. Brett still grieved over the breakup that had been instigated by the girl who wouldn't look him in the eye.

Chief Danridge took control of the gathering. "Thank you for joining us, Mandy. Let me say right off that I want to tell you how sorry I am about what happened to your father."

"A lot you know," Mandy mumbled in a whispering voice.

"I knew Vern Roberts," Danridge offered. "He helped us with the Police Athletic League football games. Ran the concession and made a lot of money for the program."

"He's dead," Mandy muttered again under her breath.

If Danridge heard her, he didn't let on. "I asked some of your friends here because I thought you might feel more comfortable around people you know, Mandy. Brett and Tara were also at the graduation ceremony when the unfortunate incident occured."

Mandy sighed, shaking her head. What did he know about the sorrow she had been facing in her life? She didn't want to listen to him. Mandy just wanted to return to the comforting shadows of her room. The darkness was more to her liking.

"I've waited awhile to question you," Danridge continued. "We had to finish our investigation before I interviewed some of the witnesses. I also wanted to give Mrs. Roberts and Mandy some time to recover.

I'll never recover, Mandy thought.

Danridge turned to Barbara Roberts. "Is it my understanding that you weren't at the ceremony that day?"

Mandy's green eyes flared under the mat of hair. "She couldn't be bothered!"

Mrs. Roberts stiffened, but she did not look at her daughter. "No, I wasn't there. I've been to several graduations, including the one where Vern was honored as teacher of the—"

Her voice cracked. She fought back the tears. She did not want to relive all the grief again, but here it came. Her lips touched the glass of liquor. She puffed at the cigarette.

Danridge looked at Coach Chadwick. "Ralph, do you remember anything unusual backstage? Anything at all?"

Chadwick's bearish face tensed. "Well," he said slowly, rubbing his chin, "it was like any other graduation ceremony. The maintenance guys set up the bleachers and the folding chairs that morning. I had to be there because I wanted to make sure they put down the protective covering on the gym floor. Otherwise, they'd tear up the—"

Danridge waved a hand at him. "Just the facts. Did you inspect the bleachers after they were up?"

Chadwick lowered his eyes. "No, that was—well, that was Vern's job. He was responsible for the sound system, too. I—I suppose that I should have helped him, but it was so busy backstage—"

Danridge leaned back. "We understand." He took a little notebook from his coat pocket and started to scribble in it.

Everyone, including Mandy, focused on the policeman. What was he getting at? Was there some shroud of mystery over the death of Mandy's father? Why did he have to ask these questions?

"Who set the wiring under the bleachers?" Danridge asked when he looked up from the notebook.

Coach Chadwick shrugged. "I guess it was Vern."

Danridge tapped his pencil on the edge of the book. "There was a two-hundred-twenty volt extension cord under the wreckage of the bleachers. But our investigation showed that all the sound equipment ran on one-ten. There didn't seem to be any need to have the cord there, but it was very close to the body. I mean to—"

Mandy glared at him. "Thanks, Chief."

"Mandy!" her mother cried.

Danridge blushed. "I'm sorry, I—"

Mrs. Roberts sighed. "It's all right."

Coach Chadwick tried to be helpful, to ease the tension. "Chief, all the lights on the stage are two-twenty. That cord could have fallen in there, when everything crashed, I mean."

"Possibly. But why was it plugged in? If Roberts was running wires under the bleachers, what was he doing with the two-twenty plug? Of course, it could have fallen in there after the bleachers collapsed. That would have caused the electrocution."

Mandy bounced quickly to the edge of her chair. "No!"

Danridge looked hopeful. "You saw something, Mandy?"

"Yes, I did," she replied. "The electricity came *before* the bleachers collapsed. I saw it. Dad was—"

Her head began to spin as the images rushed back with a nightmarish surge. The graduation day catastrophe played over in her mind. She heard the rumbling of the bleachers, saw her father twitching wildly in the power of the current. The stench of smoke filled the air. The structure crashed on her helpless father. Mandy covered her eyes and put her head down.

"It's all right," her mother said.

Danridge waited a quiet moment before his next question. "Can anyone back up what Mandy is saying?"

Coach Chadwick nodded grimly. "She could be telling the truth. By the time I got there, the electricity was all over the framework of the bleachers. I kept her from going after her father."

"Are you sure, Mandy?" the chief asked.

She looked up. "The current knocked me back. Coach Chadwick did save my life. But he couldn't save my father." She slumped in the chair again, hiding behind her bangs.

Danridge bit the eraser of his pencil. He frowned at his own notes. He seemed puzzled.

"Is something wrong?" asked Mrs. Roberts.

Danridge drew a line through something. "Those bleachers shouldn't have collapsed. According to the maintenance crew, they checked every nut and bolt that joins the framework together. They even have a list. After the bleachers go up, they have to sign off on the safety record for insurance purposes. The records show that the bleachers were perfectly sound."

"But they were going nuts in their seats," Coach Chadwick said. "They all shifted to the middle when Vern went under there. They wanted to get a look."

Danridge studied the notebook. "That's what we thought at first. But then we did our own tests, set up an identical structure. It wouldn't go down when we heaped *twice* the normal weight of a full crowd. The bleachers didn't collapse until we loosened some of the connecting bolts underneath."

Barbara Roberts frowned at the policeman. "Are you saying that the bleachers were tampered with during the ceremony?"

Danridge sighed and shrugged. "We can't be

sure. No one seems to know if your husband might have loosened something when he was crawling around under there hooking up his wires."

Coach Chadwick's face slacked into a scowl. "Impossible!"

"He was the only one who went under there," Danridge replied. "As far as we can tell, anyway. And it was his job to inspect the structure before the ceremony. Who else could it have been? The maintenance crew did everything by the book. It had to be Vernon Roberts who was careless."

The abrupt volume of Mandy's hostile voice startled everyone. "My father was never careless! He couldn't have done what you're saying. He would never endanger the lives of others!"

Mrs. Roberts slammed her glass on the coffee table, almost breaking it. "Mandy! That's enough!"

Mandy deflated in the chair, sullen and broken. "I don't care. Daddy wasn't careless!"

Chief Danridge smiled graciously at Mandy. "It's all right. I understand. We're all upset by something like this."

Coach Chadwick eyed the law enforcement official. "Chief, why don't you just come clean with us? What's up?"

Danridge grimaced. "I'm not sure."

Mrs. Roberts lit another cigarette. "I'm with Ralph on this. If you have something to say, be forthright with us."

"All right, Mrs. Roberts, I'll say it. I can't rule

out the possibility that someone might have wanted to hurt your husband."

Mandy glared at him. "No way. Who would want to hurt my dad? He wasn't that kind of person. He was good and he—"

Her face grew brighter. The anger changed to astonishment. She had forgotten all about it in the confusion. It had to be the answer!

"Jimmy!" Mandy cried.

Danridge gawked at her. "Jimmy?"

"Jimmy Boatman!" Mandy replied.

Coach Chadwick grimaced. "The Deuce?"

"He was there that day," Mandy went on. "At the gym. He was making fun of my father."

"Who is this Boatman?" the chief asked.

Coach Chadwick sighed. "One of Vern's charity cases. He's been thrown out of every school in Rockingham County. Vern gave him a last chance at Central."

Danridge wrote down the name. "I'll check it out right away. Anything else?"

Mandy was on the edge of her chair. "He was up in the catwalk, where they film the basketball games. Tara and I went up there to get a view of the ceremony. But then Jimmy came and threatened us with a knife."

"That's right," Tara chimed in. "It was Jimmy Boatman."

Brett gazed hopefully at Mandy. "I fought with Boatman. I made him drop the knife. He left after that."

Mandy did not look at Brett. "It has to be Jimmy!"

Danridge finished scribbling in his book and glanced up again. "All right, this is the kind of thing I've been looking for. Uh, if you don't mind, everyone, I'd like to speak to Mrs. Roberts and Mandy alone."

Coach Chadwick got up. "Fine by me. I don't like talking about this. It's got me spooked. Chief, if you need me, I'll be at the gym in my office." He waved and left in a hurry.

Mandy couldn't blame Coach Chadwick for fleeing. Who wanted to relive the death of her father? Mandy would have run if she had means and opportunity, even though she knew she would never escape.

Steve, Tara, and Brett were also on their feet. As they filed past Mandy, they all tried to offer their condolences. She refused to look up or acknowledge them. Why couldn't they understand that she just wanted to be alone?

Tara gave Mandy a sheepish smile. "I'll call you later?"

"Don't bother," Mandy replied. "Save your quarter."

Tara began to cry. "Mandy, please—"

Steve put his hand on Tara's shoulder. "Come on. She wants to be left alone. Good-bye, Mandy."

"That's right," Mandy snapped. "Alone."

Brett went out first, shaking his head in dismay. Steve and Tara followed him. Deep inside, Mandy hated herself for hurting them. She just couldn't stop from lashing out at everyone around her. Her wounds made her want to wound others.

When they were gone, Chief Danridge moved to one of the folding chairs. He shifted nervously, gazing into his notebook. He seemed reluctant to look at Mandy or her mother.

"What do you want now?" Mandy asked impatiently. "Haven't you done enough already?"

Her mother took a deep breath. "Mandy, let him finish what he has to say."

"Have another drink, Mom!"

"Mandy!"

The chief leaned forward. "You may not like what I'm going to say next. I'm afraid it's more bad news. Mrs. Roberts, we think that your husband may have been involved in some—well, some less than honest activities."

Mandy gaped at him. "What are you talking about?"

Danridge looked at his notes. "Well, there may be evidence that he was diverting school funds into his own private bank account. We don't have all the details yet, but the investigation—"

Mandy leaped out of her chair, pointing a finger at Danridge. "You're lying! My father would never do something like that. Never!"

Danridge started to defend his point of view, but Mrs. Roberts would not let him.

"My daughter is correct," she said coldly. "Vern would never steal from anyone. You'll never find evidence to the contrary."

The chief paused, his accusing blue eyes roving

around the ornate living room. "Tell me, Mrs. Roberts, how can you afford to live in Prescott Estates on a teacher's salary?"

"My father did lots of extra jobs at school," Mandy replied hotly. "Like helping with the graduation ceremonies."

"He was also a counsellor," Mrs. Roberts said. "And until his death, we were a two-income family. We worked hard and saved our money. *That's* how we can afford to live in Prescott Estates, *Chief* Danridge!"

Mandy scowled at him. "You're sick!"

Danridge remained calm, thumbing through his notebook. "Mrs. Roberts, your husband's life was insured for a quarter of a million dollars. Isn't that correct?"

"Yes. What concern is that of yours?"

Danridge shrugged. "Just asking. I have to consider everything."

Mandy chortled with disbelief. "How can you say things like this? How can you trash my father?"

He stood up, facing her. "Mandy, I believe that someone wanted your father out of the way for some unknown reason. I can't prove it yet, but the investigation will continue until I know the truth."

"Truth?" Mandy cried. "You're only looking for lies. Lies that will disgrace my father. Can't you leave him alone? Or do you want to shame him in his grave?"

"I'm sorry, Mandy. But we have to know the

truth. The authorities at Central are cooperating fully. I'm working with a man named Kinsley, the new assistant principal over there. We have to keep looking—"

"I don't care what you're looking for," Mrs. Roberts said abruptly. "I won't have you throwing dirt on my husband's reputation, not in his own house. Unless you have a warrant, Chief Danridge, I'll have to ask you to leave."

Danridge slipped the notebook into his coat pocket. "I can understand your anger—"

Mandy was almost hysterical. "You can't understand anything! My father was a good man. Nothing you can say will ever change that!"

A sympathetic expression came over the chief's face. "Mandy, I'm sorry that you—"

But Mandy did not want to listen to what he was saying. She ran away, tearing up the stairs to her room. She slammed the door and fell onto the bed, crying in the shadows. She could never believe the accusations against her father.

Never!

Mandy put her face in the pillow. She hated all of them for being against her. She had no one on her side.

As darkness swept over Port City, she heard the engines of the cars as the accuser left her house. It was too late now to do what had to be done. She could go first thing in the morning. She had to get away from them.

Mandy had to talk to her father.

SEVEN

Old Cemetery had been accepting departed Port City citizens since the first days of early settlement along the banks of the Tide Gate River. The rolling mound of the headland graveyard began at an iron gate on Hanover Street, rising steadily with flagging monoliths of marble and granite that served as name tags and house numbers for the coffin-bound neighborhood. Quite a few American founding fathers and mothers lay in the aged plot, keeping company with a host of other New England celebrities and local heroes. Vernon Roberts had also found his final resting place under the thick, green carpet of well-kept grass.

Mandy pushed open the iron gate, which was locked at dark and then opened again in the morning. She had been delayed at home all day. The evening sun hung low over her shoulders, casting an eerie, demon-eyed aura of orange color on the graves. She stepped slowly between the headstones, cursing her mother for making her stay around the house doing chores all day. Finally, her mother had gone out for the evening, leaving Mandy to flee in the direction of her father's cemetery plot.

Mandy stopped for a moment at the crest of the rise. She could see Newmarket Bridge from the top of the bow. The Tide Gate River ran smooth as glass under the bridge, winding into the swelling currents of Grand Bay. A gentle breeze curled in from the east, cooling the summer air. For a moment, it was all breathtaking and beautiful, but then Mandy lowered her eyes to the unweathered tablet of polished granite that marked her father's grave. He had been buried at the bottom of the slope, overlooking the river, a pretty place to call home for eternity.

Walking slowly toward the tombstone, Mandy stopped when she was close enough to read the inscription: *Vernon Roberts, Taken Too Soon*. It gave her a creepy sensation to stand over the plot. Was he really down there, six feet under? Her own father!

"It's me," she said softly. "I'm here again."

There was no reply. He wasn't going to get up and drive her home. He wasn't going to tell her that everything would be all right.

"They say you did horrible things, Daddy. They think somebody hurt you on purpose. Is it true? Is it?"

The breeze began to blow a little harder. Mandy heard thunder in the distance. A storm made noise to the east, moving in from the ocean.

"Daddy, I still love you. I—"

Mandy tried to take a deep breath. A burning sensation spread through her chest. Fear and anger welled insider her, refusing to ebb.

She threw herself on the grave, beating the ground. "How could you do this to me? How could you—"

"Mandy, Mandy, sweet as candy."

She froze, zero degrees in her bones. The voice had come from behind her. It had clearly said her name.

"Daddy!"

"Here I am, honey!"

She turned back toward the crest of the rise. A shadowed figure looked down at her. The silhouette hung motionless and menacing against the rapidly clouding sky. The shape was riding the edge of the approaching storm. It started to move toward her.

"Daddy!"

He had come back to her. She scuffled to her feet, watching the spectral figure. She reached out with her hands.

"Daddy, please, take me with you. I want to be away from here. I want to be—No!"

"I'm not your daddy, you stupid little Prescott puke!"

Jimmy Boatman's face was suddenly bright and clear. He smiled, an eely thin-lipped expression of contempt. His hands hung loosely by his sides. He stopped a few feet away from her, an oily, reptilian presence in the graveyard.

Mandy stiffened, glaring at him. "You killed my father!"

Boatman shrugged. "Maybe I did. So what?"

"You have to turn yourself in to the police!"

"No way. They got nothin' on me. They tried, but they couldn't prove a thing."

"Why? Why did you do it?"

Boatman's right hand slipped into a zippered pocket of his leather jacket. "Shut up, you little squealer. You ratted me out to the cops. Didn't you?"

Mandy ignored his accusation. "You loosened the bolts on those bleachers," she challenged. "You unplugged that cable so my father would go under there."

His eyes narrowed. The hand came out of the pocket. Mandy heard the clicking of the switchblade. The steel flashed in the evening light.

Mandy started to run, sprinting between the tombstones. Boatman came after her, screaming for her to stop. Mandy circled back toward the entrance of the cemetery. She was able to beat him to the street. She turned toward Fair Common Park, fleeing with the knife-wielding delinquent on her tail. She did not have to look back, she could hear the clomping of his boot heels.

"You're gonna pay for ratting me out," he cried. "You hear me!"

Mandy saw the common ahead of her. She had to cross the park to get back to Prescott Estates. Her legs ached, her lungs screamed for air. But she could not stop with the demon behind her.

Her green eyes kept looking for a policeman, but the streets were empty in the threat of the oncoming storm. Lightning flashed overhead. Rain began to pelt her smooth face.

The storm was emptying sheets of precipitation on her by the time she reached the park. She followed a road used by park workers. If she could reach the top of the hill, it would be a short run to Middle Street and then to Maplewood Drive. She would make it. She had to!

Her wobbly legs carried her up the incline. When she reached the top of the hill, she had to stop for a moment to catch her breath. She bent over, taking in gasps of humid air. Lightning crashed again in the dark sky. The downpour was getting worse.

Mandy rose up to run again. But she did not take one step toward Middle Street. Jimmy Boatman was there suddenly, standing in front of her with the rain dripping off his pointed nose.

She tried to turn away. Jimmy grabbed her arm, dragging her across the hill toward a huge oak tree. He slammed her against the tree, putting the knife under her chin. Lightning sliced and burned crisply above them.

"Let me go!" Mandy cried.

His breath was hot on her face. "Shut up, you little rat. I'm gonna make you sorry that you told on me."

An horrendous expression twisted his face. Boatman drew back the knife. Mandy closed her eyes. The knife thudded into the tree bark next to her ear. Boatman grabbed her face, squeezing hard.

"You Prescott types make me sick!"

"Get off me or I'll scream," Mandy cried.

He laughed hideously. "Go ahead."

Mandy screamed at the top of her lungs but no one could hear her in the storm. Jimmy pressed his body against hers, pinning her to the tree trunk. His thin fingers touched her soggy hair.

A glazed look came into his eyes. "You ain't half bad for a Prescott puke. How about a kiss?"

"You're sick."

"So, you don't want to kiss me, Mandy, Mandy, sweet as candy? Then you must want to be a loser like your daddy."

His hand grabbed the handle of the knife that was imbedded in the tree. But Mandy was not ready to give up without a fight. She lifted her knee the way her father had taught her, slamming it into Boatman's groin. He cried out and doubled over with pain, releasing his grip on the knife.

Mandy darted around him, heading down the slope. She slipped in the mud but she managed to get up again. When she looked back, she saw Jimmy Boatman staggering toward her. He wasn't running as fast as he was before she hurt him.

Feeling a new surge of strength, Mandy started to fly on more level ground. She kept looking back over her shoulder at the dark figure that grew smaller. When she reached Maplewood, she thought she was home free. She ran up the steps to her house, opening the front door and then locking it behind her.

A voice came from the kitchen. "Mandy, is that you?"

"Mom, thank God."

Her mother came into the foyer, gaping at her waterlogged daughter. "Mandy, what happened?"

"It was Jimmy Boatman," Mandy said. "He was chasing me. He—"

"Is something wrong, Barbara?"

Mandy saw the man moving in behind her mother. His auburn hair had been greased back on his head. He wore a gray business suit. Brown, narrow eyes fell on Mandy. He smiled, his thin lips parted slightly and his chin upturned.

"This is my daughter," Mrs. Roberts said. "Honey, I'd like you to meet Harlan Kinsley. He's the new assistant principal at Central."

Mandy's eyes grew wide. "I know who he is. I can't believe you brought him into this house. He's the man who's trying to—"

"That's enough," her mother said. "Be polite. I've invited him for dinner."

Harlan Kinsley flashed a leering smile. "Nice to meet you, Mandy. I just came over to tell your mother that the investigation into your father's death has been closed."

"Closed?"

"Yes, Chief Danridge believes it was an accident after all," Kinsley replied. "You see, he—"

Kinsley went on talking, but Mandy did not

hear him. Had Barbara Roberts really invited him to dinner, the man who was helping the police to besmirch her father's name? Mandy knew her mother had been spending time with some of the people from Central, but she had no idea that Mrs. Roberts had fallen in with the enemy.

"We're halting the investigation into some of your father's dealings at school," Kinsley went on. "There's no need to—"

"Shut up!" Mandy cried. "Just shut up!"

"Don't talk like that to Harlan," her mother said. "He's a guest in our home and he—"

"He's not my guest," Mandy replied. "Get out!"

"That's enough," her mother snapped.

Kinsley sighed. "It's all right, Barbara. She has a right to be angry. I know just how she feels."

Nobody knew how Mandy felt, especially this slimy creep! He had called her mother *Barbara*. Was she really on a first-name basis with this interloper? When had all this happened? In the two weeks since the funeral?

Her mother reached out for her. "Mandy—"

But Mandy no longer cared about her mother or the unwanted guest. She bolted up the stairs to her room, slamming the door, throwing herself on the bed. She felt betrayed, abandoned.

She wanted to tell someone about Jimmy Boatman's assault, but she knew it wouldn't do any good. Who would believe her? They were all against her now. And the only one who would listen could not reply. He was six feet underground in Old Cemetery.

• • •

For Mandy, the summer ticked slowly away, each passing second a moment of grief and horror. She stayed in her dark bedroom most of the time, oblivious to everything around her. She had become aware of the rumors that flew around town, stories that had her father embezzling school funds, tales that the investigation had been stopped only because her mother was chummy with the Chief of Police and Harlan Kinsley. Some said that the town did not want to smear the name of a man who had been one of Port City's leading citizens until his bizarre death.

Mandy did not care about the rumors. She knew the truth. Her father could never do anything wrong. But how was she going to clear his name when nobody wanted to believe her?

Chief Danridge had closed the case personally, so he would never listen to a sorrowful girl's story about Jimmy Boatman and his switchblade knife. Boatman had stayed away from her—so far. Why should he come after her again? He had drummed up some alibi about where he had gone after he left the gym. "The Deuce" was free and clear. He had attacked her in the graveyard just to scare her so she would keep quiet, a tactic that had worked.

Mandy felt like a prisoner in her own home. She avoided her mother and the loathsome presence of Harlan Kinsley, who had been over for dinner at least twice a week during the summer vacation. Mandy had not spoken to him once.

Coach Chadwick often accompanied Kinsley. Chadwick had tried to talk to Mandy, telling her that she should be more understanding, that her mother needed friends around her. He also urged Mandy to see her own friends, something that she refused to do. She dodged the phone calls from Steve and Tara, and the one call from Brett, who had apparently given up on her after that.

There was nothing left for Mandy except the unending sorrow and despair of her loss. She stayed in bed most of the time, watching the trees outside her bedroom window. The shadows grew longer as September approached. A few leaves began to show tinges of red and gold, the hues of autumn.

Mandy shuddered at the thought of the impending school year, which would start after Labor Day. She would have to deal with all of the expectant faces at Central Academy. What would they say about her and her father? Would they be cruel or sympathetic? Mandy thought about transferring to Rochester High, but she knew the school board would never let her leave the district where she lived. She was trapped.

When the day of reckoning finally arrived, Mandy walked to school alone, ignoring Steve and Tara who passed by in Steve's new car, offering her a ride. They tried to be friendly, but when Mandy did not respond, they just kept going, leaving Mandy by herself.

Mandy trudged up the front steps of Central to the ringing of the bell for homeroom. When she had received her schedule, she started for her first class, moving through the hall like a zombie. The other students were nice and understanding, but they kept their distance, afraid to approach the sullen girl. Mandy endured the day as best she could, her face gloomy and her eyes downcast.

When she got to the last period, she saw that Brett Holloway was in her English class. Brett smiled, trying to get her attention. But Mandy ignored him. Brett was hurt by the snub but she did not care. When the class was over, she ran off without looking at him. Mandy was comfortable with her loneliness and she intended to keep it that way.

Hurrying through the busy halls, she took the long way home to avoid seeing the gymnasium where her father had died. She thanked God that she did not have to take physical education in her senior year. She would never be able to go into the gym again.

On her way home, several cars passed and honked their horns, but Mandy did not acknowledge them. She had been lucky to have so many friends the year before, but now she had none. She didn't need friends. She just needed to be left alone so she could think of a way to clear her father's name from the horrible stories. Did they really believe Vernon Roberts was a thief?

As she approached the entrance to Prescott Estates, Mandy racked her brain for a plan, any plan as long as it brought back her father's spotless reputation. There had to be something out there that would do it. But what? And where? She started to turn onto Maplewood Drive.

"Hey, sweetness, guess who?"

The voice chilled her marrow. She lifted her green eyes to see Jimmy Boatman sitting on the brick wall that marked the entrance to Prescott Estates. She hurried past him, wondering if Jimmy would come after her. But he did not want blood. He only wanted to humiliate her.

"Yo, good lookin', Miss Perfect Prep! How was school today? I hear your daddy broke into the piggy bank. Embezzler! How's it feel to be the daughter of a thief? How's it feel, Daddy's Girl?"

Mandy broke into a run, glancing back over her shoulder once to see if he was following her. But he only laughed, pointing at her like a cruel child on the playground. He didn't have to hurt her physically, not when it was more fun to inflict psychological pain.

Running up the front steps, Mandy entered the house and turned the dead bolt. Tears flowed from her eyes. The first day at Central had been terrible. And there was no reason for her to think that the nightmare was going to get any better.

EIGHT

Large, wet flakes of December snow swirled from a gray sky, dusting Port City with an awesome layer of white. Christmas regalia festooned Congress Street and Market Square. Rows of blinking colored lights and winding garlands of metallic tinsel were strung across the width of the thoroughfare, a yuletide horn of plenty between bright store windows. Silver bells clanged in Market Square where the high bows of a spruce tree had been raised and decorated for the festivities of the season. Even the street lamps wore red bows and candy cane brooches, giving the town center the glow of a graceful noel.

Steve and Tara moved slowly along Congress Street, strolling arm in arm past the holly-wreathed line of shops. They had been going steady since Thanksgiving, one of many changes that had taken place during the fall semester. As coworkers on the school newspaper, they had spent a lot of time together before their friendship blossomed into something richer. Of course, Tara's change of heart had also been influenced by the fact that Steve had gained fifteen pounds in four months, filling out in his chest and shoulders. His extra weight and his skating prowess had gotten him a second string position on Central's all–New England hockey team. Somehow, they had become Central's most talked about couple.

Tara stopped in front of an electronics store window. She gazed in at a small, hand-held computer. It would have been the perfect gift for Mandy, even if Mandy hadn't said two words to them the entire semester.

"The Lockhart One Thousand," Steve said. "A reporter's dream. Ten-thousand-character memory and a hundred other functions. Runs on two double-A batteries. Mandy would love it."

Tara glanced dreamily at him with her huge, round eyes. "I was just thinking the same thing."

Steve returned the moony expression. "We're always on the same wavelength."

She squeezed his mittened hand with her leather-gloved fingers. Steve bent down and gave her a snowy kiss on the cheek. Tara reached up to knock a single snowflake from the end of his nose.

Tara suddenly grimaced. "Oh, we're so happy together. Why can't Mandy be happy, too! She should get back together with Brett."

Steve shook his head, frowning. He couldn't even remember why he had ever carried a torch for Mandy. Last summer, he had nursed a crush for a girl who no longer existed. Mandy had

withdrawn from everything except her school-
work and her competently written stories for the
monthly issues of the *Crier*. Steve was now the
editor of the paper because Mandy had chosen to
vacate the position.

"Poor Mandy," he said in a low voice.

"Everyone keeps hoping that Mandy will come
around," Tara went on, "but I don't think she's as
bad as people seem to think. I mean, she's getting
good grades. She's doing fine on the paper."

Steve nodded. "Yes, but what does she do with
the rest of her time? We never see her after school.
Every time we call, she gives us the brush."

"She's up to something," Tara said. "And we're
going to find out what it is, Steve. Come on."

"Wait, what're you—"

Tara blinked through the snowflakes. "Steve, I'm
tired of waiting around. And I'm sick of Mandy
rejecting us. We're going to find out what she's up
to."

"Tara, I don't know—"

"Maybe we can help her," Tara pleaded. "She
might need us."

"Is it really our business?"

Tara reached up suddenly, grabbing Steve's
face. She pulled him toward her. Their lips met in
a warm kiss.

"Okay," Steve said awkwardly. "I guess it's our
business."

Tara said, "I knew you'd see it my way. Now,
come on, let's go buy Mandy a Christmas present."

• • •

Mandy Roberts stood in front of her work desk, holding a framed eight-by-ten photograph in her hands. The color picture showed a three-year-old girl sitting on the lap of a smiling man in a Santa Claus suit. The girl was Mandy and the man in the red suit was her father. This would be her first Christmas without her father, which explained the lack of yuletide cheer in Mandy's heart.

She tossed the picture into an open desk drawer and slammed the drawer shut. Reaching into another drawer, she took out a thin reporter's notebook and opened it to an ink-smeared page. Mandy had kept her sanity by continuing her own investigation of her father's death, somehow keeping up her grades and meeting her deadlines for the *Crier*.

Jimmy "the Deuce" Boatman was the only suspect in her notes. He had practically admitted his guilt when he accosted her in the graveyard. He had been at the gym the day of the "accident" and he seemed to know his way around the infrastructure of the building. He hated Vernon Roberts, too, even though her father had been the only one in Port City trying to help him.

Mandy went over her notes. Jimmy Boatman, eighteen years old, lives on Waters Street in Pitney Docks, a rundown section of Port City. Called "the Deuce" because he was a two-time loser, spending two summers at the juvenile detention facility in Millbrook. Thrown out of Rochester High for beating up a teacher, admitted to Central under a program started by her father.

How ironic that her father was responsible for
Boatman's being at Central.

How could Boatman be so hateful as to hurt the
one man in the county who was on his side?

Mandy took a deep breath. She had been waiting
for Christmas break so that she could begin watching the delinquent. Now that vacation had arrived,
she was worried about actually going over to Pitney
Docks. She doubted she would be safe in the rough
neighborhood, especially after dark.

She had to do it, no matter what the risk. Grabbing her gloves and her stocking cap, Mandy left her
room and crept silently toward the top of the stairs.
She listened for her mother's voice. They had been
living like strangers in the big house, avoiding each
other, leaving cryptic notes instead of communicat-
ing as mother and daughter.

Barbara Roberts had been seeing a lot of Harlan
Kinsley all semester, which sickened Mandy.
Surely her mother would wake up and see
through his transparent charms. Then she would
ditch the smiling interloper for good!

Mandy tiptoed down the stairs. The phone rang,
startling her. Mrs. Roberts called from the kitchen.

"It's for you, Mandy."

She picked up the phone in the hallway. "Oh, hi,
Brett," she said blankly. "No, I'm not going to the
Christmas dance. For the same reason that I
didn't go to the homecoming dance. Uh, Brett, I'm
on my way out. Thanks for calling."

She hung up and turned toward the door.
Mandy froze when she saw her mother standing

between her and the threshold. Harlan Kinsley stood behind Mrs. Roberts with his hand on her shoulder. They were both smiling as they blocked her way to freedom.

Her mother, who had obviously been drinking, slurred her words. "Hello, Daughter. Merry Christmas."

Mandy gazed coldly at them. "I'm not celebrating Christmas this year."

Her mother frowned and pouted. "Don't be like that."

"We have a gift for you," Kinsley offered. "We'd like to give it to you now."

Mandy tried to push past them. "I told you, I'm not celebrating—"

Harlan Kinsley grabbed her arm. "Don't go."

Mandy felt an inhuman strength in his hands. She pulled back from his grasp. The doorbell rang, easing the awkwardness.

Kinsley reached back to open the front door. "Well, look who's here," he said in a jovial tone. "Your friends have come, Mandy. Steve and Tara, I believe. Come right in."

Steve and Tara came into the foyer, glancing timidly at Mandy. They had a gift-wrapped package that Tara held against her coat. Mandy was actually glad to see them. She experienced a sudden rush of guilt for the way she had treated them the past semester.

"We brought a gift," Tara said. "For Mandy."

Steve nodded. "Yeah, a gift."

Kinsley grinned broadly, a leering Santa Claus

under the mistletoe. "Tis the season. We have a gift for Mandy as well."

Barbara Roberts hoisted her drink glass. "To my daughter."

Mandy flinched when Harlan Kinsley bent forward and kissed her mother on the cheek. Steve and Tara also seemed uncomfortable. How did Kinsley have the nerve? Mandy thought.

"Perhaps we should tell her now," Kinsley said.

Barbara Roberts looked at the ice cubes in her drink. A sudden gloom had taken over her. She sipped the liquor from the glass, keeping her eyes away from her daughter.

Kinsley's arm slid around her mother's waist. "This might work better in the living room," he said diplomatically. "Shall we?"

Mandy's eyes had narrowed. "What are you going to tell me?"

"In here," Kinsley insisted.

Mandy could barely bring herself to look at his hawkish face. Her spirits had begun a free-fall toward the pit. She sensed catastrophe. Why hadn't she seen it coming? It couldn't be.

They went into the living room. Mandy fell into a chair. Steve and Tara sat on the sofa, wide-eyed with anticipation. They could feel it, too. Something big was on the way. And Mandy didn't look too happy about it.

Mrs. Roberts sat in her husband's old easy chair. Kinsley stood next to her. They were holding hands. How dare she! Mandy thought.

"Your mother and I have an announcement," Kinsley said.

Mandy's head shook slowly from side to side. "No."

Mrs. Roberts cleared her throat and straightened proudly. "Harlan and I are engaged to be married."

"No!"

Kinsley squeezed her shoulder. "We're going to make it official the day after Christmas. How do you feel about that, Mandy?"

Mandy stared straight ahead, reeling with the shock. She hadn't expected this. Her mother was betraying the memory of her father, dead for a mere six months. How could she do it?

Mandy's face turned white. She staggered toward the stairs. Her mother called after her but Mandy didn't hear. She just wanted to be alone in her room again. The lights were out again. The darkness had returned.

A bitter wind whipped through the shallow valley of the Tide Gate River, freezing the headstones in the crusty earth of Old Cemetery. Mandy stood over her father's grave, silently paying her respects. She no longer talked to Vernon Roberts. There was nothing to say to a dead man.

Something rustled behind Mandy. She looked over her shoulder to see Coach Chadwick coming in her direction. Her head snapped back. She read the words on her father's headstone for the thousandth time.

Coach Chadwick stepped up next to her. "Your mother sent me to find you, Mandy," he said gently.

Mandy shook her head inside the hood of her parka. "I'm not going to the wedding. They can't make me."

Coach Chadwick sighed and patted her shoulder. "Barbara told me to tell you that she understands. They'll see you later, after the ceremony."

"Sure. Why not?"

He glanced sideways with concerned eyes. "I know this has been rough on you, kid. Are you okay?"

She did not reply. Mandy wasn't sure about her own feelings. Inside her, there was a whirling counterpoint of confusion and numbness. The paralysis had to go away before she could recover her emotions.

Coach Chadwick's deep voice was rife with sorrow. "You're going to have to live with this, Mandy. It's going to be tough on you."

"I know, Coach. I know. I—I just can't stand to see him touch her. I don't like him. I hate him!"

"I don't care for him much myself," Coach Chadwick replied in a low voice.

Mandy looked at him with a hopeful expression. "Really. You don't like him?"

"He's too slick," the coach went on. "Moved right in on your mother. He's the kind that has to be watched."

"Tell that to my mom," Mandy replied skeptically. "Nobody can stop her from doing this."

"I'm worried about Barbara, but I'm also worried about you, Mandy."

"Me? Why?"

He looked to both sides to make sure no one was nearby. "Mandy, I've got to tell you something. But I don't want you to be afraid."

Mandy tensed, her heart pounding. More bad news, she thought. But it was best to listen if it concerned her mother and Harlan Kinsley.

"Your father was insured for a lot of money," Coach Chadwick said. "He also had another policy that paid off the mortgage after he died. With everything, your mother inherited assets worth close to four-hundred-thousand dollars."

Mandy shook her head. "I don't care about the money."

"Harlan Kinsley might," he replied gravely.

Mandy's eyes lifted suddenly to the gray steel of the Newmarket Bridge. "Of course," she said. "The money! I didn't think of that."

"I can't be sure, but he might be trying to take her for everything."

"What does anyone really know about him?" Mandy wondered aloud.

Coach Chadwick put his hands in his coat pocket. "Just be careful, Mandy. And call me if you need anything. I'm there for you. I owe it to your father."

Mandy put her hand through the crook in his elbow, locking arms. "Thanks a lot, Coach."

The bell rang in North Church, abruptly pealing through the snowy little town. Her mother was married again. Barbara Roberts had gotten herself into big trouble. Mandy had to help her.

"We missed the wedding," the coach said glumly.

"Who cares?" Mandy replied.

"You want me to drive you home?" he asked.

"No. I'd like to be alone for a while."

"Sure, I'll see you later."

When she was alone, Mandy knelt beside the headstone. She made a silent vow to herself and to her father. She would not come back to the grave as long as her mother was married to another man. She swore to stay away until she had the answers about her father's death.

Mandy lay back on her bed, staring at the ceiling, deep in thought. She was thinking about her mother who had already retired for the winter evening with her new husband. Mandy would never think of him as her stepfather. She knew that Kinsley had taken advantage of her mother's vulnerability. Her mother had always depended on Mandy's father for companionship and support. She needed those things in her life again, but she had made the unfortunate choice of the wrong man.

Mandy lifted the hand-held computer, Steve and Tara's present, to her face. It was going to come in handy now. Her investigation had grown to include Mr. Harlan Kinsley, the man who might steal the family inheritance—or even more.

Mandy loathed him. But she knew she had to pretend to be tolerant, accepting. She would watch him closely until he made a mistake.

Kinsley had been there on that fateful day of the graduation ceremony, sitting on one of the lower tiers out of harm's way. Jimmy Boatman had also been to the assistant principal's office five or six times during the fall semester, but he had yet to be disciplined. What if they were connected somehow?

Tears welled in Mandy's eyes as she entered her doubts on the computer. She hadn't even thanked Steve and Tara for the gift. She picked up the phone and dialed Tara's private number.

"Hello?"

Mandy hesitated, feeling short of breath for a moment. "Tara. It's me."

She waited for Tara to hang up on her, the way Mandy had done during the last six months whenever Tara called.

"Mandy?"

Her voice cracked. "Tara, can you ever forgive me for the way I've been treating you?"

"No problem, Mandy. All you have to do is ask."

"I need you, Tara," Mandy said. "I need your help."

"You got it," Tara replied.

"Steve, too."

"He's cool. Mandy, what's going on?"

Mandy started to tell her, catching up on their lost time, pouring her heart out. Tara listened, commenting periodically in a sincere voice. They even laughed once or twice.

They were happy to be friends again.

NINE

"Mandy, breakfast is ready!"

"Okay, Mom, I'll be down in a minute."

Mandy stood in front of her full-length mirror, turning from side to side to make sure she looked neat for school. She had chosen her red skirt and a frilly white blouse, honoring the colors of Central Academy. Her green eyes focused on the smooth face that stared back at her from the glass. The girl in the reflection had to appear happy and well-adjusted. Her alter ego wore no makeup on her pretty face, but the mirror girl had been giving a convincing, tour de force performance for the whole month of January, an act that had not been easy.

Harlan Kinsley was a tough audience. When Mandy began her jolly routine, pretending to enjoy their New Year's Eve party, Kinsley had studied her with skeptical, narrow-eyed intensity. He always seemed to be lurking about at home and at school, watching Mandy when he thought she wasn't looking. But she knew he was there. She turned at the dinner table or in the hall to catch him squinting at her, his predatory countenance tense and expectant.

The tension was practically unbearable for Mandy, but she had managed to hold up under the pressure. She thought Kinsley was probably waiting for her to show weakness again, so he could pounce on her and control her. Mandy simply refused to give him an opening. She always spoke to Kinsley in a direct manner, making eye contact, using a polite, impersonal voice. When he had requested that she call him *Harlan* at home, she complied even though the name stuck on her tongue, bringing her to call him "sir" most of the time.

Her mother was pleased by the transformation of her daughter. She had quit her job to take care of her new husband. Kinsley had treated her with respect and affection—so far. It had only been a month since the wedding. They were still like newlyweds. Kinsley doted on his wife, bringing her gifts, taking her to fancy dinners, treating her like a queen around the house. He hadn't hurt her or threatened her—yet.

Mandy figured that Kinsley was biding his time, waiting to get his hands on the inheritance. When would he make his final move? And what would he do to Mandy? She hoped to discredit Kinsley before he took them for everything. Steve and Tara were helping with an investigation that

had uncovered very little dirt on the new assistant
principal.

"Mandy!"

"Okay, Mom, I'm coming!"

Grabbing her book bag and her parka, Mandy
hurried down to the kitchen where her mother
flipped pancakes onto a breakfast plate. Mandy
sat down and reached for her orange juice. Kinsley's chair was empty.

"Where is he?" Mandy asked nonchalantly.

"He'll be here in a minute," her mother replied.

She put the plate in front of Mandy and turned
back to the kitchen counter. Reaching for a pill
bottle over the sink, she opened the cap and
popped a blue pill into her mouth, washing it
down with black coffee.

Mandy watched her closely. The pills were
something recent. Her mother had stopped drinking, but the pills couldn't be any better, unless
they were vitamins or something. And Mrs.
Roberts-Kinsley still smoked like a fiend.

A weak, nasal voice drifted from upstairs. "Barbara, where's my shirt?"

Kinsley was calling from the second-story bedroom, the one her mother had shared with Vernon
Roberts. Mandy fought off the pang that tightened
her stomach. How could her mother replace her
father with this impostor? Mandy took a deep
breath. She had to be cool, to maintain the decep-
tion at least until she could expose Kinsley for
what he was.

Her mother started for the stairs. "I'll be right back. Harlan needs me."

As soon as her mother was gone, Mandy got up and moved to the sink. She picked up the pill bottle, studying the label. She memorized the prescription name and the name of the doctor. She wasn't sure what her mother was taking, but she would find out.

"Something interesting, Mandy?"

Mandy startled, dropping the bottle into the sink. "No, I—" She grabbed the bottle and put it back on the shelf.

Harlan Kinsley stood in the archway of the kitchen. He had appeared out of nowhere, slick and smelly with the scent of his cheap cologne. His slitted eyes accused Mandy of treachery, betrayal. He came toward her, prompting Mandy to retreat to her chair.

Kinsley glanced at the pill bottle. "You shouldn't be playing with your mother's medication, Mandy. We don't want a problem like that, do we?"

Mandy's hands were trembling so she put them in her lap. "I was just looking for an aspirin."

He stiffened, glaring at her. "Do you have a headache?"

"Er, no, I—it's a personal thing, girl stuff."

"Oh."

"I'm fine, sir. Really."

Kinsley said, "You'd better hurry if you're going to ride with me."

Mandy nodded and poured maple syrup on her

pancakes. She dreaded the morning ride to school. But she had to stay close to him if she was going to catch him at something. She hoped the investigation would eventually yield a clue.

Her eyes lifted suddenly. He was staring at her. She had sensed his piercing gaze. When her eyes challenged him, he looked away. What did this stranger want from them? Why was he always staring at her like that?

"Mandy," he said in a blank voice, "I know this marriage has been tough on you. I mean, I am the assistant principal. I'm sure you've had some hard times. Other kids can be so cruel."

Mandy just shrugged. She had endured shame and indignity during her masquerade but it had not come from the other students at Central. They had been surprisingly understanding about her mother's hasty remarriage. It was almost like they felt sorry for Mandy.

Her mother glided into the kitchen with a glassy-eyed expression on her face. "Do you want pancakes, Harlan?"

Kinsley smiled. "No thank you, my love."

Gross! Mandy thought.

"I'm just having coffee," Kinsley went on. "I have to meet with the school board this morning and I don't want to feel bloated."

Her mother put a hand on his cheek. "At least let me wrap up a muffin for you in case you get hungry later."

"Whatever you say, my sweet. You're so thoughtful."

They kissed.

With the smarmy scene unfolding before her, Mandy could barely choke down the pancakes. The whole thing was maddening. But she had to stay with it if she was going to protect her mother. To help her deal with Harlan Kinsley, she kept telling herself that the investigation would reveal something sooner or later.

At the end of the school day, Mandy stood in the doorway of the room that served as the office for the *Crier*, Central's student newspaper. Her green eyes peered down the hallway, toward the library. The halls were empty. Mandy had stayed late after the final bell, telling Mrs. Wilkins that Steve and Tara were going to help her design a new layout for the *Crier*. Mandy was actually working on a student opinion column, but she really wanted to stay to give Steve access to the *Crier*'s computer.

"Where is that boyfriend of yours, Tara?"

Tara leaned against a desk, shaking her head. "I don't know. He just took off after the bell. He said to wait for him here."

"I'm going to look for him."

"Mandy!"

She hurried along the corridor until she reached the main lobby that housed Central's trophy cases. She heard voices echoing from the direction of the administrative offices. Peeking around the corner, Mandy saw Harlan Kinsley talking to a student, a boy in a leather jacket—Jimmy Boatman! She could not hear what they were saying, but she was appalled when Boatman shook hands with Kinsley. Mandy ducked back behind the wall. She heard the office door close. Jimmy Boatman's footsteps grew fainter as he went in the opposite direction.

The connection was there. Had Jimmy really helped Kinsley stage the graduation day horror? How long had Kinsley been after his goals? Since before he had come the Port City? The fiend!

A hand fell on Mandy's shoulder. She jumped and started to flail at the intruder. He grabbed her hands and pinned her against the wall.

"Mandy, it's me!"

"Steve!"

He let go of her. "Bingo," he said.

"What?"

Steve held up a slip of paper. "I've got the access code for the master computer, including Central's faculty personnel files."

"No way!"

"Way!"

Mandy's face lit up. "What are we waiting for?"

They flew back to the *Crier* office. Tara gawked as they ran in excitedly. Steve plopped behind the computer. Mandy looked over his shoulder.

"What?" Tara asked, leaning in.

"Steve got the password for the master computer," Mandy replied.

Steve's fingers glided over the keyboard. "Trudy Lawson got it for me. She works in the office where they keep the codes. By the way, she's invited to your first pool party in the summer, Mandy."

"Get the file up here," Mandy urged.

Tara clapped her hands together. "Type that puppy in."

After a few seconds, the computer file menu appeared on the screen. Steve requested the name of *Harlan Kinsley*. The data flashed before their probing eyes. Mandy blushed when she read her own address.

"Nothing," Steve said. "He has a Masters in Education from a school called Bromley in Vermont. It's an expensive private school."

"There must be something," Tara said.

Mandy pointed at something on the screen. "Look, he went to two different schools before Bromley. Maine State Teacher's College and then Florida Atlantic University. Why did he transfer so far away from the first school?"

Steve typed in *Request Transcripts*. "It doesn't say why he transferred, just that he did. Between his junior and senior year. That's weird. Most transfers are after the sophomore year, aren't they?"

"He made good grades," Tara offered.

Mandy shook her head. "Go back to his personal file."

"I'll bring up his original handwritten application for the job of assistant principal," Steve said. "Here it is."

Mandy studied the tight, precise quality of the penmanship. Harlan Kinsley had a lot of surface polish. There had to be something that did not fit in the perfect pieces of the puzzle.

Her eyes scanned the pages. "Look, personal reference. Dr. Otto Beekman. That's the name on Mom's prescription. Kinsley is giving her some kind of pills, a tranquilizer. I looked it up this morning in the library."

Tara's eyes bulged from her head. "Oh my God. Check it out."

Mandy followed the pointing finger. "What have you—no! I don't believe it."

Steve read it aloud. "Marital Status: *Widower*!"

"Does your mother know he was married before?" Tara asked.

"I don't know," Mandy replied, "but she's going to find out."

"I wonder how his wife died." Tara pondered.

"It doesn't mat—"

Mandy had turned toward the door. She almost cried out when she saw Harlan Kinsley standing in the open doorway. His arms were folded over his chest. How long had he been standing there? What had he heard?

Tara grabbed Steve's shoulder. "Hello, Mr. Kinsley!"

Steve pressed a button that cleared the computer screen. "How's it going, sir?"

A stern expression covered Kinsley's face. "You're working awfully late. Do you have permission from Mrs. Wilkins?"

Mandy nodded, trying to forget the butterflies that fluttered in her stomach. Her legs were like rubber. She knew she had been caught. What would Kinsley do to her now? What would he do to her mother?

Tara responded quickly to cover for Mandy. "We're working on a new layout for the *Crier*. It's going to be great."

Kinsley kept his gaze on Mandy. "How late will you be here?"

Mandy shrugged. "I'm not sure."

Kinsley took a couple of menacing steps toward the computer, craning his neck to stare at the bare screen. "Looks like you haven't made much progress."

Mandy smiled nervously. "I wouldn't say that."

Kinsley's expression was disapproving. "I'm working late, too. Can you get a ride with Steve and Tara?"

"Yes, sir."

His head moved in a semicircle. He glanced at each one of them with the guile of an assistant principal. The look was meant to instill guilt in them. Without another word, Kinsley wheeled on the balls of his feet and walked out.

"He knows," Tara said glumly.

"Maybe," Mandy replied. "Steve, do you think it'd be too risky to bring up that file again?"

"Don't have to. I sent it to the printer in the other room. All you have to do is press a button and you've got hard copy."

Tara started for the print room. "Do it. I'll tear the sheets."

Mandy patted Steve on the shoulder. "Excellent. I wish we could get some more information on him."

Steve reached into a drawer. "Maybe we can. I'll call Maine State and hook up. It's just on the other side of the state line."

"Can you hack into a university computer?" Mandy asked.

"No, but I can call the library computer. It's part of a regional information-sharing program. I've done it before with other schools."

"Do it!" Mandy said. "Now."

Steve called the library at the college and hooked into the information system. There was no direct file on Harlan Kinsley, so they went through old issues of the school paper, focusing on the year before Kinsley transferred to the school in Florida.

"Hey, this might be it," Steve said.

Mandy read the headline. "Student Faces Plagiarism Charge Before Honor Council. Harlan Kinsley! There it is."

Steve pushed the right button. "Hard copy."

"I'm on it," Tara rejoined.

Mandy read on a little further. "It says here that he was also in trouble during his sophomore year. Three times he was arrested for disturbing the peace! He has a criminal record!"

"More hard copy," Steve said. "Be sure you show this to your mother."

"Tonight," Mandy replied, smiling, "as soon as I get home."

• • •

"Mom?"

Mandy stuck her head into the kitchen. Her mother sat on a stool, talking on the telephone. Mandy called again, prompting her mother to wave. Mandy stepped back into the hallway, pacing back and forth, bursting to reveal the evidence that would finally free her mother from the philanderer who had come into their lives. Surely her mother would see the truth in the light of real evidence from Kinsley's own record.

She thought her mother would never get off the phone.

Finally, she hung up and came into the hallway. "Mandy, how are you, dear? Did you ride home with Harlan?"

"No, Mom. Listen, I've got something to tell you. It can't wait. It's about Har—"

A key clicked suddenly in the lock of the front door. Harlan Kinsley pushed in from the cold. His eyes immediately fell on Mandy and her handful of computer printouts. He was tense for a moment but then he smiled when he saw his wife.

"Barbara, sorry I'm late. I had a problem at school. Somebody keeps trying to break into the Central computer files."

Mandy felt her spirits sinking. He was looking right at her. He knew. Would he tell her mother all about it?

Her mother threw her arms around her new husband. "Harlan, I'm so glad you're home. The papers came today. I want you to sign them as soon as possible."

"We can talk about it later," Kinsley replied coolly.

"What papers?" Mandy asked.

"Just legal stuff," her mother replied. "I'm putting Harlan on my bank accounts and my investment portfolio. He's going to handle all the financial dealings from now on."

Kinsley actually blushed. His face turned bright red. Mandy glared at him. He was caught but there was nothing she could do to stop him from putting his hand in the cookie jar—not yet anyway.

"We can talk about this later," he said impatiently.

"Okay," her mother replied in a happy tone. "Mandy, didn't you have something you wanted to say to me?"

Mandy's stomach did a back flip into an empty pool. "I—"

Kinsley leered at her. "Yes, by all means, tell us, Mandy."

But the brown-haired girl was speechless. She could not confront him with her mother there. She'd have to bide her time, and catch her mother alone in a more receptive mood.

In the meantime, the wolf was free to roam in the meadow with an unsuspecting sheep . . .

TEN

Mandy vaulted over the stairs, two at a time, fleeing to the sanctuary of her locked bedroom. Leaning back against the door, she hugged the sheets of incriminating paper. Kinsley knew she was gathering evidence against him. His reference to the school computer was proof of his suspicions. Mandy wondered if he was also aware of Steve's call to the Maine State College library. It was a cat and mouse game with Mandy trapped in a corner. When would the hungry feline devour her?

The evidence had to be hidden. Now that he knew she had it, Kinsley would surely come looking for it. But where would she be able to hide it? The only box that locked was her jewelry case.

She dumped all of her jewelry into a drawer and then folded the pages into small squares. The wad of paper barely fit into the jewelry box. She closed it with a healthy shove and turned the key in the lock. The box fit neatly in the bottom drawer of her dresser, behind piles of socks. It would have to do for now.

Voices reverberated in the hallway outside her room. Mandy pressed her ear to the door. Kinsley and her mother were talking. They went into her father's old study. Mandy heard the door open. They were no doubt going to sign the papers that would give Harlan Kinsley control of everything her father had left them.

"How can she?" Mandy whispered to herself.

She had to talk to someone who would understand.

Easing into the hallway, she gazed toward the door of the study, which was slightly ajar. Light spilled into the hall from the study. A shadow blocked the light for a moment. Mandy held her breath, thinking that Kinsley had heard her. He was going to catch her in midflight.

But the door closed with a smart rap. Kinsley wanted complete privacy to work his dirty dealings. Mandy stole out of the house quietly, emerging into the winter night.

A gray sky hid the crescent moon. The air was tainted with swirls of wood smoke from Port City's chimneys. Mandy ran until her lungs started to ache from the cold. She was walking briskly by the time she reached the entrance of Prescott Estates. She turned to her right, heading for Middleboro, the next neighborhood over, where Coach Chadwick lived.

The sidewalks were fairly clear of snow so she was able to make it to Chadwick's place in fifteen minutes. He lived in a private home, renting a small garage apartment with only one bedroom, boasting that a career bachelor did not need a lot of frills to exist. He prided himself on a Spartan life-style, except for pizza and other take-out food.

Mandy climbed the steps to his doorway. She pounded frantically. Coach Chadwick answered the door clad in a red Central T-shirt and sweat-pants.

"Mandy, what're you—"

"Coach, please let me come in. It's an emergency."

"Sure."

Coach Chadwick let her in, offering her a seat at a tiny dinette table. Mandy sat down. Her hands trembled on the table top.

Coach Chadwick landed on the other side of the dinette. "What is it, Mandy?"

Mandy shook her head. "She did it. Mom signed over everything to Kinsley. They're doing it right now."

Coach Chadwick grimaced and slammed his fist on the table. "How could she do that to *us*?"

Mandy grew hopeful. "Us? You mean you're with me?"

He nodded, patting her hand. "You bet, kid. I couldn't let your father down. I'm with you all the way."

"What can we do?"

He sighed, his bear face wrinkled in thought. "We have to get something on him, something that'll stick."

She told him about the evidence they had gathered on the computer. Chadwick was impressed, especially with the knowledge that Kinsley was a widower. But he figured that wasn't enough. If they presented the evidence and her mother rejected the truth, they would never be able to get her away from Kinsley. They needed something better than misdemeanor arrests and unproven allegations of plagiarism.

"If I could just tell Mom—"

"No!" Chadwick said. "I mean, not yet. It would just scare her. Or make her more resolved to stay with him."

Mandy wrung her hands nervously. "Coach, I'm afraid. What's he going to do to us?"

"Stay calm," he told her. "And call me if there's trouble. In the meantime, keep looking for something we can use against him. Something good."

She nodded sadly. "Oh, Coach, I miss him so much. I wish he was here."

"It's been a nightmare for you, Mandy. For all of us who liked your dad."

"Will it ever be over?"

Coach Chadwick stood up. "You better get home. Don't leave your mother alone with him. Keep your eyes open, Mandy. Run if it gets too tough."

"I will, Coach."

"Come on, I'll drive you."

"Okay, but let me off on Middle Street. I don't want him to see you."

He put his hands on her shoulders. "Call me, okay? Promise."

"I promise."

Mandy hugged him. She felt a lot better about having the coach on her side. Maybe together they could stop Harlan Kinsley's evil handiwork.

The house on Maplewood was dark as Mandy approached the front steps. She entered cautiously, listening in the silent darkness. Kinsley and her mother had retired early. Mandy did not want them to hear her before she reached the safety of her room. She had to take the steps slowly in the darkness.

At the top of the staircase, Mandy stopped dead, gazing toward the thin shaft of light that spilled into the hallway from her father's study. Were they still awake?

Mandy stepped slowly toward the light. Maybe her mother was alone. Maybe Mandy could talk some sense into her.

"Mom?"

She pushed on the door. There was no reply from the study. A lone desk lamp illuminated the warm enclosure.

Mandy entered the room, peering toward the oak desk that had belonged to her father. The desktop was thick with piles of paper. Mandy moved behind the desk, thinking there might be a clue among the documents.

As she shifted through the paper, her heart palpitated and sweat formed on her upper lip.

Most of the papers were written in complicated legal jargon that Mandy could not understand, stuff from the lawyer, the broker, and the bank. There wasn't anything to help her investigation.

Her green eyes caught a flash of dark blue between the stacks of paper. It was her mother's checkbook. Mandy had never pried into the financial affairs of the family, but she had to take a look. She opened the register, scanning the entries.

Her face went slack. "No way!"

The last entry read: *Harlan Kinsley, $14,000.*

Her mother had written the check that very night! Why was she giving him so much money? It was blood money for her father's life. Kinsley the vampire was going to drain them dry.

"Studying a little late, aren't you, Mandy? Even for a Friday night."

She dropped the checkbook. Her eyes lifted to the figure of Harlan Kinsley who stood in the doorway with his arms folded over his robe. He peered down his long, narrow nose.

Mandy's lips quivered with the hasty reply. "I-I was looking for a pencil. I—"

Kinsley said, "Did you find one?"

Mandy stood up. "I'd better be going." She started for the door.

Kinsley blocked her exit for a moment. "You don't have to snoop around, Mandy. If you have a question, just ask."

She shook her head, barely getting out the words. "No, I-I just wanted a pencil."

"Are you sure that's all you want?" he asked accusingly.

She raised her head, looking him right in the eye. "Are you going to let me out of here? Mom!"

He said, "Don't wake her. There's no need."

He stepped aside.

Mandy brushed quickly past him, running for her room. A blast of cold air hit her as soon as she opened the door. The window was up, allowing the winter wind to blow through her bedroom. Mandy locked the door and then secured the window. She switched on a light.

"What in the world—"

Someone had been in her room. The place had been wrecked. Someone had searched the drawers of her dresser. Her jewelry box lay in the middle of the floor, smashed into pieces. The intruder had stolen the papers that she had hidden in her dresser.

The words formed on her lips. "Harlan Kinsley."

Then she caught sight of the mirror from the corner of her eye. The name was scrawled awkwardly across the glass in magic marker: *The Deuce.*

Jimmy Boatman had done it. He *was* working with Kinsley after all.

A surge of adrenaline coursed through Mandy's body. What was she going to do? If she called the police, they wouldn't believe her. They'd dismiss her as a grieving girl with an overactive imagination.

She picked up the phone, hoping Kinsley was

not on the extension, and dialed frantically, she waited breathless, until her best friend picked up after two rings. "Tara, it's me. I know it's late, but I had to talk to you."

"Mandy, what's wrong?"

Mandy choked back the tears. "Something has happened. I have to get out of here. Would it be all right if I came over?"

"Sure. You want to spend the night?"

"Yes, if it's all right."

"Tomorrow is Saturday, Mando. No prob."

"Thanks."

"Are you walking?" Tara asked.

"Yes."

"Be careful, Mandy. It's late."

Mandy hung up and started to pack an overnight bag. Tara lived ten blocks away on the other side of Prescott Estates. Mandy figured she'd be safe there for the night. They could decide what to do about the investigation. Something had to give sooner or later. They had to establish proof of Kinsley's guilt.

Mandy went downstairs, leaving a note for her mother. She didn't want her mother to worry. Even Kinsley couldn't say anything about her spending the night at a friend's house, especially on a weekend.

As soon as she was outside, Mandy raised the hood of her parka to ward off the bitter wind that whipped down Maplewood. She started for Tara's house, hearing strange things in the night, pray-

ing that Jimmy Boatman had left the neighborhood.

The old Ford Fairmont rolled north on the
interstate, winding between steep, snow-covered
slopes that were dotted with evergreen trees and
bare limbs. Steve was behind the wheel of the blue
four-door bomb that coughed smoke and belched
sparks from the tail pipe. The car was an early
graduation present from Steve's parents, as well
as a Christmas and birthday consideration since
they weren't exactly rich. It wasn't much to look at
but it got great mileage and the heater even
worked.

Tara sat close to Steve in the front seat. She
seemed worried. Tara was not sure about the road
trip to Vermont, even though Mandy had made it
sound right the night before.

Mandy was stretched out in the backseat. She
had talked them into leaving early, before day-
light. She didn't want her mother and Kinsley to
know that she had gone out of town. If they were
lucky, they could be back by noon with the evidence that Mandy needed. Maybe she could find
what she was looking for in Vermont. Her eyes
read the welcoming sign as they crossed the state
line.

Steve yawned. "What time is it?"

Tara looked at her watch. "Seven-thirty."

Mandy moaned and rolled her eyes. "Steve!"

"Are you okay?" Tara asked.

"I just want to get this over," Mandy replied. "Can't you go any faster?"

Steve shrugged. "If I get a ticket, I lose the car," he replied. "We'll be there in ten minutes. Chill out, Mando."

Mandy sighed. "I'm sorry."

Steve looked at her in the rearview mirror. "Hey, it's cool. I understand. Kinsley is something to worry about. Making your mom sign those papers."

"And the fourteen thousand dollars!" Tara said. "What about that? The rat is stealing from her already."

"I still find it hard to believe he's working with the Deuce," Steve said. "Major surprise on that one."

Mandy gazed thoughtfully at the drifts of snow. "I know. I wonder if they were working together from the start? That would make Kinsley the one who killed my dad."

Tara shuddered. "I hate him!"

They were quiet until Steve pointed to the sign. "Here's the exit."

Mandy read it aloud. *"Bromley, This Exit. Bromley College.* This is it. Harlan Kinsley's alma mater."

They came off the exit, turning toward town. For a moment, Mandy was able to gaze down into the shallow valley. The sleepy little town spread innocently before her, resting in a dark bed of morning shadows, ready to be awakened by the truth.

ELEVEN

Steve's breath made a fog trail in the cold morning air. "What a bummer."

Tara hooked her arm through his, guiding him away from the Bromley College library. "Two hours in that place and we couldn't find a thing about Harlan Kinsley."

Mandy walked behind them with a perplexed look on her smooth face. "It's like no one at this school wants to admit that he exists."

Steve had used one of the library terminals to try to hack into the computer files of the registrar's office. But they didn't have the password code and they couldn't get it because the registrar was closed on Saturday. The investigation was off the beam again. It seemed hopeless.

They ambled past the ivy-trimmed brick buildings of classrooms and dormitories. Bromley was a quaint New England college known for its academic excellence and high tuition. Rich kids usually went to Bromley.

"I wonder how Kinsley could afford to go here?" Mandy pondered aloud.

"Maybe he didn't," Tara offered. "Maybe you caught him in another lie."

Steve shrugged. "Who can tell? Come on, let's go back to town and have some hot chocolate."

Tara glanced at her watch. "It's not even ten o'clock. We can still buy breakfast. I have money."

Mandy exhaled a dejected column of fog. "Why not? We've struck out."

They left the campus, strolling along a tree-lined street. Traffic was fairly heavy in the town center. With the school and the close proximity to skiing country, Bromley was a busy little place on this freezing Saturday.

Mandy kept shifting her eyes about, looking back and forth, watching for some sort of clue. She wondered if Kinsley had actually trod the very street that took her into town. What had he done to make the school want to forget him? Was there anyone left in Bromley who knew Kinsley?

Tara drew closer to Steve. "This is a cute little town. Let's settle down here when we're married."

Steve bristled at the joke. "Forget it. I'm never getting married. Hey, there's a place. Let's eat breakfast. I'm starving."

Mandy stopped in the middle of the sidewalk. She saw another building ahead of them on the same side of the street. The Bromley Public Library was only a couple of doors away, a neat, white clapboard structure with a huge clock over the entrance.

"You coming, Mandy?" Steve asked.

Mandy shook her head. "You guys go on, I'll join you in a couple of minutes. I want to have a look at the local library."

Tara seemed concerned. "Are you sure?"

"Go on."

"See you in a few," Steve said.

Steve and Tara started across the street for the Fife and Drum Restaurant.

Mandy hurried on the salty sidewalk. She knew the library was a long shot, but she had to try. Most local librarians kept tabs on regional news, focusing on the noteworthy activities of home folks.

The clock above the entrance began to clang ten o'clock as Mandy approached. She found the librarian ready to lock the front door. The matronly, gray-haired woman turned to glare at Mandy.

Mandy tried to look hopeful. "Please, Ma'am, I'd like to come in for a few minutes. Just a little while."

The woman adjusted her wire-rimmed glasses and gave Mandy a disapproving scowl. "We're closed."

"But—"

The woman's wrinkled finger pointed to the sign on the door. "Saturday, eight to ten in the morning, thanks to the budget cuts. We keep it open mostly for book return. Do you have a book you want to return?"

"No," Mandy replied. "I need some information."

"You'll have to come back on Monday."

She started to close the door.

"But wait," Mandy persisted, grabbing the door handle. "I'm from Port City. I *can't* come back on Monday."

The librarian remained stubborn. "Rules are rules, young lady. If I broke them for you, I'd have to do it for everyone else."

"Please—"

"Sorry! Now let go of the door."

Mandy held fast to the handle. "You don't understand. I need to know about someone. A man named Kinsley, Harlan Kinsley."

The woman's jaw fell and she dropped her keys. "Harlan Kinsley?"

"Yes, Ma'am."

The woman let go of the door. "What's Harlan Kinsley to you?"

"He married my mother," Mandy replied in a sorrowful tone.

"Pick up those keys and follow me."

Mandy scooped up the keys and followed her through a small foyer that opened onto a larger room that smelled of old books. The woman pointed toward a table in the reading area, ordering Mandy to take a seat. As Mandy sat down, the woman disappeared into the shadows of the bookshelves.

An electric current flowed through Mandy's body. Could this be it? Did the woman really know about Harlan Kinsley?

The librarian returned, waddling to the table.

She had a photocopy with her. She put the paper in front of Mandy.

"Is this what you're looking for, young lady?"

Mandy read the headline of the news story. "Wife of Student Killed on Mount Adams." The student was Harlan Kinsley.

"Happened a long time ago," the librarian said softly. "They were up there to celebrate his Master's degree. He graduated in the fall semester."

"His first wife," Mandy said. "Was it really an accident?"

The librarian frowned. "That's what the paper says. And the police agreed. They found her wrapped around a tree trunk. But around here, we know different. It was the money that made him take her to Mount Adams."

A picture of the high peak accompanied the newspaper story. Mandy had never been to Mount Adams. It was a ski area near Cooperville, about twenty miles north of Bromley.

The gray-haired woman leaned over the table with the enthusiasm of a gossip. "His first wife came from money. Everybody knew it. They say her family paid his way through school. That's the only reason he married her. Then there was some court action after she died."

"Court action?"

"Rumor is that Kinsley sued her family for his right to her inheritance. I heard he got a hundred thousand, but some say he didn't get a penny."

"And they never arrested him?" Mandy asked.

"No. He went free without a charge. They couldn't prove a thing. He's a slick one."

Mandy sighed. "So he's going after my mother now. He's slick all right."

"What?"

Mandy tried to muster a smile. "Nothing. Could you please make a copy of this for me?"

"I certainly will, young lady. No charge!"

The librarian receded from sight between the bookshelves, disappearing again. Mandy felt a sense of triumph. She had stuck it out and now she had just what she needed. Harlan Kinsley had more than likely killed his first wife, even if it could not be proven.

Now her mother had to listen.

By half past noon, Steve had them back in Port City. He turned the car onto Maplewood, rolling toward Mandy's house. She had told them everything on the ride back.

"Are you sure you don't want us to come in with you?" Steve asked.

"I'm sure," Mandy replied.

Tara glanced back at her with a genuine expression of concern. "He might be dangerous."

Mandy shook her head. "No, I've got him now. He won't dare make a move with this much evidence against him. He has to be cool now that I know the truth. He won't try anything."

Steve braked in front of her house. "Good luck."

Mandy opened the back door. "I'll call you."

"Be careful," Tara warned.

Mandy closed the door and watched them drive off. They were good friends. They had come through for her when she needed them.

Mandy braced herself. She had to face her mother. She would also call Coach Chadwick as soon as she had presented the evidence to Mrs. Roberts-Kinsley.

She has to believe me now, Mandy thought.

When she entered the house, Mandy saw a pair of suitcases standing in the hallway. Her hopes soared. Maybe Kinsley was already on the way out. He knew Mandy had the goods on him. He was taking an early flight out of their lives, the wolf fleeing the shepherd's threat.

"Mandy?"

Her mother's voice came from the living room. Mandy rushed in to find her on the sofa with a drink in her hand. Mandy took the drink away and then knelt in front of her mother.

"Mom, you have to listen to me—"

"I'm all right, Mandy, give me back my drink."

Mandy grabbed her mother's wrist. "You're not going to hide behind alcohol this time. You have to listen."

"Mandy, what's wrong with you?"

"It's Kinsley," Mandy replied. "He's bad news, Mom. His first wife was killed on Mount Adams."

Her mother stiffened and looked away. "That was an accident. Harlan told me all about it. She broke her neck while she was skiing."

"That's not what they say in Bromley," Mandy challenged. "He killed her and then sued her family for her inheritance. He also has a police record and he was thrown out of Maine State for cheating."

"Mandy, you know none of this is true."

"He's a skunk, Mom! He's after your money now. You can't trust him. You have to tell him to leave this house."

"Mandy, I won't listen to any more of this slander about your stepfather. Do you hear me?"

Jumping to her feet, Mandy began to pace back and forth. "He's not my stepfather! Can't you see what he's doing?"

"That's enough!"

"Mom!"

Her mother reached for a pack of cigarettes.

Mandy knocked the pack off the coffee table. "Stop it! Stop hiding behind your vices. Listen to me, Mom. You're in danger!"

"Harlan has never treated me like anything but a lady. He's kind and good. All you can do is say bad things about him."

"He's a liar from hell, Mom. He's moving in for the kill. He had this boy, Jimmy Boatman, take stuff from my room. They're working together against me. I think he also had something to do with Dad's dea—"

Her mother stood suddenly. "Hello, Harlan. We were just talking about you."

Mandy thought she had turned to stone. She was frozen in her shoes. She sensed Kinsley's dark presence behind her. He moved around slowly, sliding next to her mother, putting a hand on her shoulder.

Kinsley had a worrisome twinkle in his eyes. "I hope you were saying good things about me. Where have you been all day, Mandy?"

Mandy took a step backward. "Nowhere."

Kinsley eased his arm around her mother's waist. "Oh? Didn't you take a ride with Steve and Tara this morning?"

She blushed. He knew. He was playing the cat again. Mandy had to maneuver around him.

"Where did you go?" he asked.

"I-I don't know. Just riding."

Her mother grinned drunkenly. "Let's all be happy. Just for one day. A big happy family."

Mandy moved sideways, slowly heading for the hall. She wanted to get away from Kinsley. She had to call Coach Chadwick. He would be on her side. He would know what to do next.

"Where are you going?" Kinsley asked.

Mandy hesitated. "Uh, to my room."

Kinsley smiled at his wife. "Tell her what we have planned, Barbara."

Her mother giggled like a dutiful wife. "Oh, Harlan. You're so romantic. He thinks we should have a vacation, Mandy. We haven't been any-where since we got married. It's like our honey-moon."

"But it's Saturday," Mandy challenged. "How far can you go? You have to be back by Monday."

Kinsley shrugged, casting his steely gaze on Mandy. "We can take Monday off. We want you to come with us, Mandy. I mean, I'm sure the assistant principal won't mind if you miss one day of school. Ha. Ha-ha." He began to laugh in a disturbing chant.

Mandy knew she had to stall. "Uh, I haven't packed yet." She wanted to get to a telephone.

"I packed for you," her mother replied. "Everything we need is in those two suitcases."

Kinsley kept leering at her. "You don't have any excuses, Mandy. Why don't you come with us? We'll get you a separate room. You like to ski, don't you?"

"I can't," Mandy said. "I mean, I don't want to go."

Kinsley urged her mother toward the front door. "Well, if you don't want to go, I suppose it will just have to be the two of us, Barbara. It will be our honeymoon celebration."

"Will you be all right?" her mother asked.

"Mom!"

They brushed past her, going into the hallway. Kinsley picked up the suitcases. Her mother opened the front door and went out to the car.

"Where are you going?" Mandy demanded of Kinsley.

"Why, to Mount Adams," he replied nonchalantly. "It's beautiful up there this time of year."

Mandy's skin began to crawl.

Mount Adams!

Kinsley was taking her mother to the place where he had killed his first wife. He wasn't wasting any time. He planned to murder Barbara Roberts-Kinsley in the same way.

"Are you sure you won't come along?" Kinsley asked cryptically.

Mandy couldn't let her mother go alone. "All right, I'll come."

Kinsley turned toward the front steps. "Let's get moving. We don't have time to waste."

Mandy reached for the hall phone. "I just have to make one call."

He gazed back over his shoulder, his eyes wild and bright. "No calls. If you tarry, we leave without you." He went down the steps.

Mandy quickly dialed Tara's number. There was no answer. She had probably gone over to Steve's. Mandy dialed Steve's place but the line was busy.

The car engine revved outside.

Kinsley honked the horn.

Mandy wanted to call Coach Chadwick, but she heard the car backing out of the driveway. She had to hang up. If she didn't hurry, they would leave without her. Her mother would be all alone with Kinsley on Mount Adams.

Mandy put down the phone. She ran out of the house, chasing the car along Maplewood. Kinsley stopped to let her in.

Mandy climbed into the backseat, huffing and puffing, trying to catch her breath. "I'm going with you."

"Good," her mother said. "We're glad to have you."

Mandy's hand was trembling as she closed the door.

Kinsley's face glanced back at her in the rearview mirror. "You won't regret coming along, Mandy. You're going to love the mountains of Vermont."

She had jumped right into his trap.

He stepped on the gas, rushing them to their doom.

"Oh, we're going to have so much fun!" her mother said.

We'll be lucky to escape with our lives, Mandy thought.

She found herself heading north on the interstate, retracing the route she had taken earlier that day. Mandy had to protect herself and her mother from the madman behind the wheel of her late father's Toyota.

But how?

She had to think of something before they reached Mount Adams.

TWELVE

When the Toyota sped past the Bromley exit on the interstate, Mandy leaned forward and spoke to Kinsley over the top of the seat. "Bromley College. Didn't you get your Master's there, *Harlan*?"

Kinsley cleared his throat, glancing back and forth with nervous twitches of his head. "I—yes, I did go there, Mandy. You should know." His hostile eyes glared at her in the rearview mirror.

Mandy fell back, retreating from his gaze. His face was taut with a fretted brow. He looked frazzled, like a scared, desperate animal. Was he reliving his heinous deeds in anticipation of performing them again on Mount Adams? Did he really think he could get away with it a second time?

Her mother leaned against the window on the passenger side, dozing in a stupor. Mandy was frightened, terrified, but she knew she had to protect her mother. The fear provided her with the alertness of a stalked prey. She had to be ready for Kinsley to try something.

"Why were you asking about Bromley?" Kinsley said nonchalantly.

Mandy tensed. "I-I was thinking about going there. How was it?"

His eyes flickered in the mirror. "You should know. You went there this morning with Steve and Tara."

A slicing pain cut through Mandy's stomach. Kinsley knew. And he was initiating the cat and mouse game. He wanted to play with her before the ax dropped. He was crazy.

Her mother sat up, weaving in the seat. "What? Mandy came to Bromley? When, Mandy?"

"Uh—"

Kinsley laughed uneasily. "Nothing, dear. Just a little joke between us. Isn't that right, Mandy?"

Mandy thought the flash flood of fear would levitate her from the seat. Her entire body vibrated. Was this how it felt to face death? Kinsley wasn't going to let her live, not after her mother was gone and he had all the money.

Why had she come at all? She could have stayed home, used the telephone. No! She could not leave her mother alone with this madman.

The sign on the road read: MOUNT ADAMS 15 MILES.

What was she going to do?

It had to be quick.

Get away from Kinsley, find a phone, call Coach Chadwick. If she was going to the police again, she wanted an adult on her side. Even if the

authorities could not arrest Kinsley, the hassle
might be enough to make him back off a little. He
wouldn't dare try anything with the police watching. Her mother would just have to sober up and
face the truth eventually. Mandy could never stop
trying as long as Kinsley darkened their home.

The car rolled on through the dull afternoon
light that reflected and diffused an orange color in
the snow-dusted valley. Mandy kept running over
the plan in her mind. Get away, make the call,
wait for Coach Chadwick to arrive. She could also
call Steve and Tara. She knew the number of her
mother's phone credit card, so the long distance
charges wouldn't be a problem.

She held her breath when they passed the exit
sign for Cooperville. A sign pointed the way to the
Mount Adams Ski Area. Kinsley guided the car
down the ramp. Mandy felt paralyzed. It was like
the dream where she could not move. Only this
was really happening.

Kinsley turned the car toward Cooperville.
"We're staying at the Snowdrift Inn," he said in a
calm tone. "It's on the other side of town, sort of
isolated, but the lodge has its own lift."

The shift of tone had Mandy puzzled. She
leaned forward until she found the angle; his face
loomed in the rearview mirror. Kinsley was stable, composed, almost serene. The nervousness
had somehow left him. Something else had taken
over his entire being. Had the monster surfaced
now that he was back on his old stomping
grounds?

They drove through the pleasant little town, which was buzzing with the weekend skiers. Mandy saw the bus stop. She could always get away on the bus. No! She could not think of escape. She had to protect her mother.

The road left town, winding through a wooded area of thick evergreens. Mount Adams towered over them, a snow-capped giant blocking the sun. They broke out of the trees and headed for a long, wooden structure at the base of the mountain. The Snowdrift Inn would have been paradise for anyone else, but Mandy saw it as a dangerous place. How was she going to free them from Kinsley?

Her eyes lifted to the smooth white slopes. A ski lift rose behind the lodge, following the mountain to a substation on a plateau above the inn. Skiers rode the I-bar to the top, swooshing back down on what had to be the beginners' run. The skiers were desperately trying to take advantage of the last rays of afternoon light. It would be dark on the mountain in another hour. Mandy wondered if Kinsley had killed his first wife at night.

The Toyota ground to a halt in front of the office. "I'll check in," Kinsley said.

Mandy started to open her door. "I need some air."

Kinsley shook his head. "No. Stay here. I'll get the rooms. Then we're going to talk, Mandy. A long talk. It's way overdue."

No way! Mandy thought.

Kinsley got out of the car and went into the office.

Mandy leaned forward, shaking her mother's shoulders. "Wake up!"

Her mother stirred and said dreamily, "Harlan's so nice."

She was useless, zonked on pills and whiskey.

Mandy's eyes scanned the area for help. She saw a line of pay phones running along one side of the building. She started to get out. Kinsley turned inside, gazing at her through the frosted window. Mandy closed the door.

She'd have to sneak away later. She hoped the coach was home. There was no other course of action.

Perspiration broke on her forehead. A chill spread through her shoulders, following the sweat. What if this was all for nothing? Kinsley could just plead innocence. He hadn't really done anything to hurt them.

It didn't matter. She had to keep making noise until her mother saw the light. She had to ring the bell, sound the alarm.

Kinsley returned to the car, not saying a word. He steered the Toyota to the other end of the lodge. He wanted to be away from everyone. Did he plan to do it right there?

He took the bags up to their rooms and then returned to help her mother climb the stairs. Barbara Roberts-Kinsley swayed and stumbled. Kinsley was going to make it look like an overdose! It was so clear now.

Kinsley hesitated in the doorway, looking at Mandy. "Are you coming?"

Mandy tried to smile. She wanted to make it seem natural, like she was ready to accept the weekend outing. This might be her only chance to break away from him. It had to be right.

"I'm thirsty," she said casually. "I'm going to look for a soda machine. I'll be right back."

"Mandy, I think—"

She darted away, heading for the next entrance to the lodge. Entering the heart of the inn, she followed a long corridor to a dining room. The office was on the other side. Mandy found her way across the dining room which was starting to fill with early diners.

A pay phone hung on the wall of the office, but Mandy didn't want anyone to hear her. She headed outside to the line of phones along the wall. She had to pick up three receivers before she found one that worked. It was a rotary phone, so she had to give the numbers to the operator.

The coach's phone seemed to take forever to ring. He didn't answer. She had the operator try the number again but Coach Chadwick was not home.

"Tara."

After a few moments, she got the operator again. Tara's phone rang. She picked up on the other end. But before Mandy could speak, a hand reached past her, disconnecting the call.

She turned to look at Harlan Kinsley's tense face.

"What are you doing?" he demanded.

"I'm running!" Mandy cried.

She pushed him hard. Kinsley stumbled backward. His feet hit a patch of ice and he went down.

Mandy ran for the other end of the lodge. She had to find someone to help her. Kinsley called after her, but she just kept going, sprinting as fast as the weather would allow.

A brittle pain spread through her chest as she rounded the far corner of the inn. She had to stop for a second so the aching would subside. She glanced back toward Kinsley, who was now on his feet. He started after her. Mandy had to hide. But where?

Her green eyes found a set of wooden steps that rose to a plateau behind the inn. The sign read: LIFT; an arrow pointed the way up. Mandy had to hold the handrail as she mounted the stairs, fleeing the demon on her tail. She was out of breath by the time she reached the top step.

A narrow wooden walkway stretched toward a planked structure. The ski lift still moved in the dimness through it was now empty of all riders. Mandy could hear the groaning mechanism from the plank building. Maybe there was a place to hide around the lift.

"Mandy, come back!"

Kinsley's strident voice echoed through the shroud that darkened the valley. An eerie yellow light from the west illumined the higher slopes of Mount Adams as the sun died. Mandy ran over the wooden walkway, making for the murky angles of the lift housing.

The long conveyer belt of I-bars moved steadily

through the substation. A few skiers dotted the beginners' slope, winding in from a great day of sport in the snow. Some of them carried torches, forming swiftly cascading embers of fairy light in the purple-washed trails. Mandy loved to ski, but she now thought only of saving her life.

Mandy came onto the platform where skiers boarded the lift. The motorized whirring of the mechanism was much louder. Her eyes followed the line of I-bars to the substation above. Was there a phone up there? And if she rode the lift, would she be able to get down again?

"Mandy, where are you?"

Kinsley was not ready to quit. She heard the echo of his feet on the wooden steps below. There had to be some place for her to hide. She saw the door with the CAUTION sign painted across it. She tried the knob and found that the door was unlocked.

"Mandy, don't run away."

Kinsley was at the top of the steps.

"Mandy, please!"

Mandy ducked into the dark enclosure without him seeing her. The room housed the whirling machinery of the lift. Mandy locked the door easily from the inside. She started to search for a weapon.

"Mandy!"

Kinsley had crossed the wooden path to the platform. He was outside the door. Mandy saw the ski pole leaning against the wall. She picked it up and held it in front of her.

"Mandy!"

She backed away from the door. Kinsley kept calling her name. Something grabbed her parka from behind. The huge wheels and gears of the lift turned and grinded, tearing away a hunk of nylon fabric. Mandy gasped and then put her hand over her mouth. She jumped back, unharmed but petrified.

Had Kinsley heard her?

She could not detect his footsteps anymore. She moved back to the door, pressing her ear against it. A sudden pounding sent a shockwave through her head. Kinsley's fist banged again.

"Mandy, are you in there?"

She held her breath as he tried the doorknob.

"Mandy, you don't have to be afraid. I brought you up here so we could all talk. Mandy, are you in there?"

Closing her eyes, she prayed for him to disappear from their lives.

"Mandy, come out. I won't hurt you. It's all right. I promise I won't do anything to harm you."

No, Mandy thought, you'll just *kill* me!

He cursed under his breath when she did not answer. Mandy thought she heard him walking away, but she could not be sure with the noise of the lift's machinery. After another ten minutes, she peeped through the cracked doorway to see that the platform was empty.

Mustering her nerve, she moved away from the jaws of the machinery, using the ski pole as a lance to fend off any attack from Kinsley. But he had abandoned the chase, at least for now. He was nowhere to be seen in the shadows.

Mandy swallowed a deep breath of icy air. She had eluded Kinsley for the moment, but there wasn't any time to waste. She had to use the phone before he caught up to her. This time she would call from the office so there would be people around if Kinsley tried to make a scene. He'd have to behave in front of eyewitnesses.

She retraced her path on the wooden walkway. If she could just get to the phone, she could try Coach Chadwick again. Maybe Steve had hung up by now. She had to talk to someone. Then it would be all right.

Before she reached the steps, Mandy slowed, gazing down the second walkway that led to the other end of the lodge. Kinsley had probably followed the second walk, so it was better for her to go down the steps, taking the exact same route back to the office.

At the top of the steps, she stopped again, gazing into the eyes of an unexpected player in the game. He was standing on the third step down, smiling at her. His hands were tucked into the pockets of his leather jacket.

"Mandy, sweet as candy."

His hot breath fogged the frigid air.

"You!" Mandy cried.

Jimmy "the Deuce" Boatman had appeared from nowhere. He had followed Kinsley to Mount Adams, no doubt to help his boss. They really *were* working together.

Boatman started to take a step upward. "Don't worry, Miss Candy. I'm not goin' to hurt y—arh—"

Mandy had swung the ski pole, catching Boatman in the side of the head. Boatman screamed, teetering a moment before he lost his balance. He tumbled backward, crashing down the steps.

The ski pole felt heavy in her hands. She gazed at the fallen body below. Blood seeped from a gash on Boatman's forehead. For a moment, she thought she had killed him. She started to take a step down so she could help him.

"No!"

Jimmy Boatman stirred, trying to rise. He managed to stagger to his feet, still reeling from the blow. Mandy saw the knife blade flash as it appeared in his hand. Boatman did not need her help.

She had to run.

Her aching legs carried her over the walkway again. She could have gone in the other direction, to the opposite end of the lodge, but she figured Kinsley was there, looking for her. They had surrounded her, closing in from all sides. There was only one way to go if she wanted to escape.

When she returned to the platform, Mandy climbed onto the lift, riding the I-bar up the slope. The narrow seat would carry her to the substation and the beginner's run. Maybe there was a phone above.

Mandy clung tightly to the bent ski pole, wondering if Jimmy Boatman had enough strength to follow her.

THIRTEEN

Icy rushes of air breezed by Mandy's face as she flew upward into the gray shades of dusk. The sunlight was almost gone, leaving only a dull crest of yellow on the summit of Mount Adams. Mandy swung quietly in the seat, watching the substation grow larger. She kept looking back over her shoulder to search for Jimmy Boatman. But it was already too dark to see the lower seats and the lodge had become a black shape in the valley. The evening would have been peaceful, if not for the terror in her heart.

The lift dropped her in the snow. Her seat swept into the substation, coming out on the opposite end of a platform to allow a return trip for beginners who couldn't muster enough courage to ski down. Mandy trudged a few feet in the snow to get to the platform. The entire structure of the substation was dark. She started forward with the sharp end of the ski pole leading the way.

The place had been abandoned for the night.

144

Mandy felt her way along the outer wall, searching for help. The doors had been locked at the pro shop where skiers rented and purchased equipment. A CLOSED sign hung in the window.

Mandy heard something behind her. She wheeled to see a skier whizzing past the substation. He was a straggler, trying to get home before dark from one of the higher runs. Mandy called to the speeding figure but she could not be heard.

What was she going to do?

She had to keep moving. If she did not find help, she would ride the lift back to the lodge. Maybe she could stay one step ahead of Kinsley.

As she started along the wall again, automatic security lights glowed to life overhead, responding to the signal from a timer. Mandy could see better in the silvery sheen. The signs were clear to her when she turned the corner again.

REST ROOMS.

TELEPHONE!

A slight recess in the wall held the pay phone and twin doors for the rest rooms. Mandy slipped into the alcove, leaning the ski pole against the wall. She dialed the operator. She made herself repeat the numbers slowly, fighting the urge to panic and scream. She wanted to be understood.

Coach Chadwick's phone rang twenty times but he did not answer. She had to call Tara. The operator took forever to come back. Finally Tara's phone rang in Port City.

"Hello?"

Mandy sucked cold air into her aching lungs. "Tara, thank God!"

"Mandy?"

"Yes, Tara—"

"Mandy, it doesn't sound like you. Are you all right?"

"Tara, listen, please! Kinsley is going to hurt my mother. You've got to find Coach Chadwick. Tell him to meet me at the bus station in Cooperville."

"Mandy, call the police!"

"Tara, I can't do that, not until the coach gets here. Now listen, you've got to find him. Sometimes he goes to the YMCA on Saturday to—"

"Put down the phone, Mandy!"

She froze with the receiver to her ear.

Kinsley's voice penetrated the shadows of the substation. He stood at the entrance to the recess, blocking Mandy's chance of escape. She was cornered.

"Hang up," Kinsley told her. "Now."

She dropped the phone, leaving it to dangle freely. "Tara, he's after me. Call the police!"

Kinsley came toward her, grabbing the receiver. "You little fool."

"Tara, I'm at Moun—"

Kinsley ripped the receiver cord out of the pay phone. Mandy tried the rest room doors but they were both locked. The ski pole still leaned against the wall. Mandy picked it up and lifted it to drive Kinsley back.

"Put that down!" he demanded.

She waved the pointed end at him. "No! You aren't going to kill me. I'll fight back."

Kinsley's body seemed to deflate. "What? Kill you? Mandy—"

Mandy's anger overcame her other sensibilities, even the fear. She hated this man. He had ruined her life. She had to confront him with his own lies.

"I know all about you," she said in a hostile voice. "You were arrested. You cheated. Plagiarism! You copied someone else's work so they bounced you out of Maine State!"

Kinsley folded his arms. "Then it was *you*. You're the one who hacked into the school computer. But you've got it all wrong, Mandy."

"Why were you arrested then?" she challenged.

Kinsley shook his head. "Nothing serious. I was hauled away three times for protesting the nuclear power plant at Leabrook. There was a whole group of us."

Mandy's father had been to similar protests, but that didn't matter. "What about the plagiarism charges? You were thrown out of school!"

"I was cleared of that. Another student switched papers with me. He confessed later."

"You changed schools. Why?"

He sighed. "I was angry. I—it wasn't the most mature decision. But then I met—"

She jabbed at him with the pole, forcing him back. "What about Jimmy Boatman? You had him take stuff out of my room. He's here now. Isn't he?"

She could not detect the concerned expression

on his countenance. "Boatman? Mandy, I don't know what you're talking about. I would have thrown Boatman out of Central last semester if Coach Chadwick hadn't told me about your father's outreach program. I was just trying to show respect to your dad."

"Respect? The way you moved in on my mother—"

"I know it seemed quick," Kensley replied, "but I never knew your father. And I fell in love with Barbara. I *am* in love with her, I swear. She's the first woman I've loved since my first wife."

"The wife you killed!" Mandy accused.

His body straightened with a sudden jerk. "You little—Mandy, I've been patient with you up till now, but I don't have to take this."

"You killed her!" Mandy cried. "Everyone in Bromley knows it. You killed her and sued her family for her money."

Kinsley kept silent for a moment.

"Admit it, *Harlan*!"

"Wow," he replied in a low voice, "those gossips in Bromley really got to you."

"Murderer!"

"Get off it, Mandy. I never hurt her. And I never took one cent of their snooty money. Just ask them. Get *all* the facts before you make a judgment."

"You took them to court!"

"They sued *me*!" Kinsley cried. "They wanted me to sign a paper saying that I wouldn't make any claim on the inheritance. I signed it in the judge's chambers. The trial was over in ten minutes. I never saw them again."

"How could you afford to go to Bromley then?" Mandy asked.

"Student loans. It took me ten years to pay them back. But I did it. I don't owe anything to anyone."

They were silent for an awkward moment. Mandy thought he sounded too convincing. *He's slick. A slick one.*

"Mandy—"

"No, you got my mother on tranquilizers! They came from your doctor!"

He shook his head. "No, Barbara went to the doctor behind my back. I'm trying to get her off the pills, Mandy. I swear. I had her off the liquor until today. That's one of the reasons I wanted you to come with us. We can confront her together, make her stop."

"You want the money!" Mandy ranted. "You had her write a check for fourteen thousand dollars. You wanted a taste before you grabbed the whole jar of cookies!"

Kinsley slumped again, hanging his head. "Yes, I don't deny that check was for me. But the money was for something I'd rather not talk about."

Mandy smiled triumphantly. "I'll bet!"

"No, it's not like that—"

"Then why did you take the money from her?"

He sighed deeply. "Mandy, that check was meant to repay money that your father embezzled from school funds. He was stealing, Mandy. I found the records myself, in his office."

"Liar!"

He took a step toward her. "Mandy, I swear, I'm telling the truth."

She raised the pointed end of the pole to his eye level. "Stay away from me or I'll blind you."

"Your father *was* stealing, Mandy. I suppressed the evidence when your mother agreed to reimburse the entire sum from her inheritance."

"The inheritance you tried to steal!" Mandy replied. "Mom give you control of everything."

Kinsley's voice grew softer. "I refused to sign those papers, Mandy."

"Liar!"

"Ask your mom," he went on. "I tore up those documents right in front of her. I don't want any of your money. I love your mother, rich or poor. I think she loves me. I don't expect you to care about me, but I would like it if we could at least start getting along."

She waved the pole in a tight circle. "Get out of my way."

"Mandy—"

"If you're really telling the truth, then you'll let me go!"

He hesitated. "I—we—Mandy, I—"

"Out of my way!"

Kinsley sighed again. "All right."

He stepped aside.

Mandy could not believe him. "All the way

back," she said. "Go on. Just leave me alone if you really don't want to hurt me."

"Mandy, let's ride down together."

She shook her head. "No way. You get lost. Get out of here. Go back to Port City. I want to be alone with my mother."

"Mandy, please—"

"It's the only way I'll believe you," she challenged. "Go!"

Kinsley threw up his hands. "Have it your way, Mandy. I'll see you back in Port City. But hurry down to your mother. She needs you, Mandy. She needs *us*."

Kinsley darted away, leaving Mandy in the shadows of the recess. Did she dare believe him? No! It had to be a trick. She waited for him to return but Kinsley did not come back.

The pay phone had been torn apart by Kinsley, so Mandy had to go back to the lodge to make her call. Leading the way with the ski pole, she eased out of the recess, half expecting Kinsley to attack. A dull squeak made her jump, but it was only the sound of the lift mechanism grinding away over the platform.

Mandy walked a slow circle around the substation. As she came onto the platform for the lift return, she saw Harlan Kinsley standing there under the spectral silver of the security light.

Kinsley was not alone. Another male figure stood to the side, in the shadows. When he stepped forward into the circle of pale radiance, Mandy saw the man's bearish face.

"Coach Chadwick!" she cried.

Dropping the ski pole, she ran to the burly man, throwing her arms around him for a warm hug.

"Where did you come from, Coach?"

Chadwick's voice had a lackluster tone. "Been following you all day."

She finally felt safe with Chadwick there. "Oh, it's been horrible."

Kinsley glared at them. "You two teamed up against me?"

Chadwick glared back at him. "Shut your stupid mouth, Kinsley. You scared this girl half to death."

Mandy's green eyes flashed angrily. "Yes, half to death."

Kinsley turned toward the lift. "I've had about enough of this drivel for one evening. I'm going to see my wife."

Coach Chadwick lifted his right arm. "No, Kinsley. You're staying here. You're not going anywhere."

Kinsley's eyes grew wide. "You wouldn't!"

"Yes, I would," Chadwick replied.

Mandy gasped when she saw the gun in the coach's hand. "Coach, call the police. You don't have to—"

"Hush, Mandy," Chadwick replied. "We're gonna settle this right now."

Mandy drew back a little. "Be careful, Coach. You don't have to shoot him. Take him to the police."

"It was you!" Kinsley said suddenly.

"Shut up," Chadwick told him.

Mandy wanted to grab the gun. "Coach, please. What are you going to do?"

Before Chadwick could reply, another voice rang through the night air.

"Heyyy. What's up. Shuh! Mandy, sweet as candy."

Jimmy Boatman moved up behind Kinsley, edging into the light.

"Watch him!" Mandy cried. "They're working together, Coach."

But Boatman did not stop next to Kinsley. He kept walking toward Chadwick and the gun. He didn't seem to be afraid of the pistol.

"He has a knife," Mandy warned.

Boatman put his hands on his hips. "Hey, Coach! You caught these Prescott pukes. Just like you said you would!"

FOURTEEN

Mandy frowned at Coach Chadwick whose dull eyes were locked on Jimmy Boatman. The Deuce kept grinning like he and the coach were old friends. Mandy looked back and forth between them, wondering what was happening.

"Yeah, the coach is somethin' else," Boatman went on in a slippery tone. "He wanted to be your daddy, Mandy. Ain't that a good one?"

Chadwick pointed the gun at the smiling delinquent. "Shut your hateful mouth, Deuce."

Boatman ignored the pistol, stepping back to put his arm around Kinsley's shoulder. "Yo, Mr. Assistant-principal puke. Girly-girl here thought you was out to get her. Only it was Coach behind the misery."

"I said to shut up," Chadwick warned through gritted teeth.

Mandy eased away from the man with the gun in his hand. "Coach, what's he talking about?"

"Nothing," Chadwick replied quickly. "He's just blowing off steam. He's crazy, that's all."

The Deuce laughed and swaggered toward Mandy. "We're all crazy. Hey, Miss Prescott. How you think we got here? Huh? Accident? Me and the Coach-man been doggin' you for two days. Who you think it was took the stuff out of your room?"

"No," Mandy mumbled. "It can't be."

"I took it," the Deuce went on. "Me. Yeah! See, we been tryin' to frame old Kinsley here, but you loused it up by running away. Only it's better now, cause we got everyone here. Ain't that right, Coach?"

Chadwick's expression was hard, cynical. "I'm warning you to shut up, Boatman. Shut your loud mouth."

The Deuce ignored him. "Hey, we can make it look like Mandy-Candy killed the principal here. And then she killed herself. Or is it the other way around? I forget. What's it gonna be, Coach?"

Chadwick looked at Mandy. "Don't listen to him."

"What's he saying?" Mandy asked, her body shivering. "Didn't you come here to help me, Coach?"

Chadwick smacked his dry lips. "It's more complicated than that, Mandy."

The Deuce cackled like an old warlock over a cauldron. "Complicated? You bet. Real complicated."

"I don't like this, Coach," Mandy said.

"It's not what he's saying, Mandy. It's not like that."

"Not like that?" the Deuce railed. "Then tell me why you had me pullin' bolts on graduation day,

Coach Baby? Shuh. Why'd I plant that frayed extension cord to light up old Vern? I'll tell you why! So Mr. Roberts goes under the bleachers! Zzt! Boom! He's buzzard bait!"

"No," Mandy said softly. "Coach couldn't do that. My father was his friend. He couldn't—"

"He did!" Boatman rejoined. "Big time!"

Kinsley took a step forward. "Chadwick, am I correct in assuming that you were the one who planted all that embezzlement money in accounts that were listed under the name of Vernon Roberts?"

Chadwick shook his head. "You've got it all wrong."

"Just as I suspected," Kinsley replied. "There's your truth, Mandy."

The Deuce had another hearty laugh. "Whoa, that's it. Coacherino! Opened a dummy account to smear Mandy's daddy, only Kinsley saves the day by lettin' the drunk mother pay it all back. Keeps everything quiet so the widow will owe him. That's when Coach decided to set up Mandy. Put her against her new father so they'll kill each other and Coach has the drunk mommy all to hisself!"

Kinsley shook his head, sighing, "You know, Boatman, I should have thrown you out of Central when I had the chance."

The Deuce made an obscene gesture. "No way, Principal Prescott Puke. I had to stick around to help Chadwick kill you."

"No!" Mandy cried.

Chadwick's finger tightened on the trigger. "That's enough, Deuce!"

The switchblade appeared in Boatman's hand, reflecting the silver rays of the security lights. "She's gotta pay for hittin' me in the head, Chadwick. She's mine, you hear."

Kinsley started at Boatman. "Leave her alone!"

The Deuce dissuaded him with the knife. "Stay outta this, pig! I'm gonna have some fun before I cut her." He turned back to Mandy, his eyes wet and glassy.

Mandy retreated slowly. "Don't do it, Jimmy!"

Boatman showed her the blade. "It's already done, Mandy-Candy."

He began to stalk her.

The pistol exploded suddenly in Chadwick's hand. Boatman cried out and grabbed his stomach. He fell into the snow, wrestling himself in agony.

Mandy glared at the coach. "You *are* a killer!"

Chadwick gawked at her. "I had to do it, Mandy. He was going to hurt you. I have to protect you and Barbara. You're all I've got."

"You don't have anything," Kinsley said.

Chadwick scowled at his rival. "You! You ruined everything."

Mandy held out her hands. "Give me the gun, Coach."

"I can't," Chadwick replied. "Not until you let me know where you stand, Mandy. You can have it either way."

Mandy squinted at him in the spectral light. "Where I stand?"

He smiled weakly. "Don't you see, Mandy? I did it for *us*. For you, me and your mother. I knew I could treat you right."

Mandy shook her head. "You really did it," she said blankly. "How could you? How—"

"Vern had everything," Chadwick replied, "I had nothing. We were the same age, but he had your mother, a big house. Nobody wanted me. But I knew I could make your mother happy once he was out of the way."

Mandy started to say something until she noticed Kinsley's movement from the corner of her eye. He was inching toward the ski pole that she had dropped on the platform. The coach didn't seem to be aware that Kinsley had stepped over the squirming figure of Jimmy Boatman.

Mandy knew she had to keep Chadwick distracted. "Coach, mother never wanted you. She loved Dad. Turn yourself in while you still have a chance."

His face slackened into a frown. "You're wrong, Mandy. Barbara loves *me*! We can be a happy family. You, me, your mother. I love her. I love you, Mandy. I want to make both of you happy. I want to be your dad."

Mandy almost felt sorry for this raving lunatic. "How?" she challenged in a firm voice. "How can we be family, Coach?"

His expression grew hopeful. "We can do it. All you have to do is go along with what you were saying before. We can frame Boatman and Kinsley. We can say *they* did it. I saved you from them. I'll look like a hero. Your mother will love me even more. Then it'll be the three of us. Nobody has to know what really happened."

She shook her head. "I'll know."

"Mandy—"

"No way, Coach."

A pitiful gleam came into his eyes. "Then I have to kill both of you, Mandy. I'll have to make it look like the Deuce killed you and then himself. You're a bad one, Deuce."

Boatman moaned in the snow. Kinsley stood next to him, within easy reach of the ski pole. When Chadwick glanced in Kinsley's direction, the thin man knelt down, as if he was trying to help Boatman.

Chadwick exhaled a column of fog. "I'll have to finish Jimmy. He's still alive. What a day."

He turned the pistol on the groaning delinquent.

Kinsley and Mandy exchanged glances with Kinsley nodding.

"Okay," Mandy said quickly. "I'll go along with you, Coach."

Chadwick lifted his eyes from the wounded boy. "What?"

"Now!" Kinsley cried.

Mandy dived for the platform, hitting belly-down.

Harlan Kinsley swung the ski pole, striking Chadwick's wrist. The gun went off but the bullet missed Boatman. Chadwick dropped the pistol and grabbed his hand. Kinsley swung the pole again, catching the coach in the knee.

Chadwick did not go down. Instead, he moved back toward the gun. Mandy beat him to it, sweeping the pistol from the platform.

"Give me the gun!" Chadwick cried.

Mandy held it on him, even though she had never fired a pistol in her whole life. "Please, Coach. I don't want to hurt you."

Chadwick took a step toward her. "Mandy—"

She ran to the edge of the platform, slinging the pistol as far as she could. The gun landed in the deep carpet of snow, disappearing. Chadwick would never find it in the dark.

His bearish face twisted into the mask of a madman. "You little idiot."

Kinsley held the ski pole like a baseball bat. "That's it, Chadwick. You're finished."

But Chadwick went after Mandy anyway.

She teetered on the edge of the platform, standing under the rising I-bars of the lift. Chadwick closed in with his arms outstretched. But before he could grab her, his head jerked back and his body shook.

Chadwick wheeled around to face Kinsley who had hit him in the head with the ski pole. "I'm gonna kill you first!" Chadwick cried.

The odd twist of fate now prompted Mandy to fear for the life of the man she had hated. Chadwick had fifty pounds on Kinsley. But Kinsley had the ski pole and he was neither a weakling nor a coward.

"You!" Chadwick cried. "All becau. I'm going to tear out your throat."

"Stop now," Kinsley said. "I don't wai. you."

Chadwick wasn't listening. He charged headlong. Kinsley raised the pole like a jousting lance, rushing forward to meet the charge. The point of the ski pole caught Chadwick in the middle of the chest. He grunted and stumbled backward, but he did not fall. He reeled and teetered under the belt of I-bars, keeping his balance at the edge of the platform.

"Quit now!" Kinsley said. "Give it up, Chadwick!"

"Gonna kill you both!" Chadwick cried.

Chadwick lunged at Mandy this time. Kinsley had no choice. He charged with the ski pole, slamming Chadwick with full force. The blow knocked the burly coach from the platform into the snow. Chadwick moved to stand up again, still bent on revenge.

"You're dead, Kinsley! You hear me. Dead—what!"

As Coach Chadwick started to rise from the snow, one of the I-bars caught the back of his heavy coat. The ski lift jerked him from the ground. His arms and legs kicked but he could not free himself.

"Help me!" he cried, uttering his last words.

Mandy and Kinsley jumped from the platform, grabbing at the coach's dangling legs. But they could not free him either. It was too late.

The I-bar carried him upward, dragging Chadwick into the whirling wheels and gears of the lift mechanism. His inhuman cries echoed through the calmness of the dark valley. Mandy covered her ears so she would not hear the crunching of bones and cartilage.

Suddenly the lift ground to a halt. Some of the twinkling lights went dead in the valley. Mandy stood there motionless and silent. They were both in shock. Kinsley dropped the ski pole and started back toward the lodge.

There was nothing left to do but call the police.

Mandy sat on the edge of the bed in her mother's room at the lodge. She held a cup of lukewarm hot chocolate in her cold hands. Her mother sat next to her, sipping coffee with a befuddled expression on her face. Unlike her daughter, Mrs. Roberts-Kinsley wasn't exactly sure what had happened on Mount Adams, not yet anyway.

The truth had been hard on Mandy. She was numb again inside. It was almost like her father had died a second time.

Her mother touched Mandy's hand. "Honey—"

"Shh," Mandy replied in a whisper. "Listen."

Voices rose in the hallway outside the room. The state police had been called to investigate the incident. Nobody had sorted out all the details. Mandy wondered when they were going to question her. She came off the bed, moving closer to the voices, listening through a cracked door.

". . . and you say your stepdaughter threw the gun from the platform. Is that correct, Mr. Kinsley?"

Kinsley's tone was low and exhausted. "Yes, that's correct."

"Mr. Kinsley, I'm sorry, but I'm going to have to arrest you for manslaughter and for attempted murder."

Mandy could not believe what she was hearing. "No!" she cried, pushing her way into the hall. "He didn't do it!"

A tall policeman was cuffing Harlan Kinsley. "Sorry, miss. We have to arrest him. He's been in trouble before up here. We can't just let him go."

"But you don't understand," Mandy replied. "He didn't do it. The coach was the one. And Jimmy! Ask Jimmy Boatman. He's still alive!"

"Boatman is in a coma," the trooper offered. "He's been taken to Mount Adams Memorial Hospital. As soon as he wakes up, we'll talk to him. In the meantime, you have the right to remain silent . . ."

Mandy appealed to some of the other troopers, but they did not want to listen to an hysterical girl. They were just doing their job. They had to arrest Kinsley.

As they were leading Kinsley away, he turned to smile at Mandy. Once she had wanted to see him dragged off in handcuffs. But now she knew that she had been wrong. Kinsley had saved her life. He didn't deserve to be punished for something he didn't do.

Her mother came into the hall. "Harlan? What happened to Harlan?"

"It's okay, Mom."

"Where are they taking him? What's wrong?"

Mandy sighed and put her arm around her mother's shoulders. "They're taking him to jail, Mom. But don't worry. We're going to get him out. I promise, Mom. I promise."

Mandy sat by the hospital bed, gazing at the pale face of Jimmy Boatman. Boatman had been in Mount Adams Memorial for three days, unconscious, in a sleep of death. Harlan Kinsley had spent the same number of days in the Cooperville jail, held without bond.

Boatman's torso had been wrapped in ghostly white bandages. The bullet had done some damage to his insides, but he would probably live after the surgery. Mandy kept wondering when he would wake up. Jimmy could straighten out everything with a few words.

She took his hand, gently patting his palm. "Wake up, Jimmy. You can do it. Come on."

A male nurse appeared behind her. "I'm sorry, miss, you'll have to come back tomorrow. Visiting hours are over."

Mandy looked over her shoulder. "A few more minutes. Please."

"Well, I—hey, look. Well, I'll be. Maybe I will let you stay a few more minutes. You're good for the patient."

Mandy gazed at Boatman again. His slitted eyes were half open. He looked at her and moaned.

The nurse started to leave.

"Stay!" Mandy said. "I may need you."

"Sure," the nurse replied.

Mandy held Jimmy's hand. "Hello," she said softly. "Jimmy, who made you pull the bolts on graduation day? Who made you do all those horrible things?"

Jimmy mumbled something. Mandy leaned in to listen. She called the nurse over.

"Listen to him," Mandy said. "What's he saying?"

The nurse bent over. Mandy repeated the question to Jimmy. His lips barely moved.

"I can't hear," the nurse replied.

"Closer," Mandy insisted. "Say it, Jimmy. Who made you do all those horrible things?"

Boatman's words were a little more precise.

Mandy smiled at the nurse. "Did you hear that?"

"Uh, yes, I think so."

"What did he say?" Mandy asked. "Tell me."

The nurse shrugged. "It sounded like 'Coach Chadwick' to me."

Mandy clapped her hands together and jumped to her feet. "Thank God."

"Where are you going?" the nurse asked.

"To get the guard outside this room," Mandy replied. "It's time to call the state police and get my stepfather out of jail!"

EPILOGUE

Graduation day was almost over. Mandy chose to skip the ceremony at the Central Academy gymnasium, despite graduating with honors. Even though it had been a year since her father's death, she still could not bring herself to attend the commencement in that same building. The assistant principal, her stepfather, had excused Mandy from the ceremony. She would receive her diploma in the mail.

Mandy sat alone on the edge of the diving board. Port City was in for another hot summer, prompting an uncovered pool in the backyard of the house on Maplewood. Mandy basked in the June sun, peering into crystal water, thinking about everything that had happened to her in the past year.

Admitting Kinsley's innocence had been a difficult adjustment for her. Her stepfather had been a victim of circumstance and poor timing. He really seemed to be a loving, devoted husband to her mother. Kinsley had actually persuaded her mother to give up drinking and smoking. After some family counselling, Barbara Roberts-Kinsley was holding her own. Mandy had tried to be understanding, but they had been walking on eggshells since the tragedy at Mount Adams.

Mandy sighed, lifting her eyes to the clear June sky. Kinsley had worked hard to clear her late father's name. No one in Port City believed the horrible rumors now. All the money had been returned to the proper sources, leaving the reputation of Vernon Roberts intact. Maybe, Mandy thought, it was time to start giving Kinsley a break.

She kicked her bare foot in the water, thinking about Ralph Chadwick. Who could have known the darkness in his troubled heart? He had pretended to be a family friend so he could kill her father. Who could have known?

A shiver played across her back. Mandy had not gone to the coach's funeral. Few people had attended the final rites for the hateful deceiver. One of Port City's most respected citizens had become a monster overnight. At least Chadwick had left no family behind to bear his legacy of deceit and shame.

The bell ran in North Church, clanging five times for the hour. All over Port City, graduation parties were underway. Mandy felt somewhat left out, even though she knew it was her decision to stay home. Had she made a mistake in isolating herself?

"Mandy?"

She turned her head to see her mother standing at the back door. "Hi, Mom. I'm okay."

Mrs. Roberts-Kinsley came out of the house carrying a portable phone. "It's Brett, honey. Do you want to talk to him?"

Brett had been so sweet in the last months of the school year. He had asked Mandy to the prom. Despite her refusals, Brett kept trying.

Mandy reached for the phone. "Hi, Brett. No, I can't go to a party. But if you want to stop by later—you will? Okay. See you."

She handed the phone back to her mother.

"Everything okay, honey?"

Mandy nodded. "Brett might be coming over later."

"That's wonderful!"

"Sure."

Mrs. Roberts-Kinsley returned to the house. Mandy sat there, brooding, hoping that Brett would really stop by. She actually wanted to see him.

"Mandy?"

Harlan Kinsely's voice startled her. He stood at the back door.

"Oh, hi," she said blankly.

He smiled. "I just came from the ceremony. Everyone missed you."

She sighed. "I'm sorry I didn't—"

"I understand," he said sympathetically. "I just brought over some people over who wanted to see you."

Steve and Tara emerged from the kitchen, stepping around Kinsley.

Mandy's face broke into a grin. "Hi, guys."

Steve carried three pizza boxes. "Party hearty. Pizza on your stepfather. Oh, I-I mean—"

Everyone seemed embarrassed by Steve's reference to Kinsley.

"It's all right," Mandy said. "He's my stepfather. It's okay."

Kinsley nodded and went back into the kitchen.

Tara winked at Mandy. "We knew you really didn't want to be alone today."

"How was graduation?" Mandy asked.

Steve shrugged. "Not bad." He started to dig into a pizza box.

Tara rolled her big eyes. "Not bad? It was hot and horrible. I hated every minute of it."

Mandy gazed into the pool. "You don't have to say that just because of me."

"I'm not," Tara insisted. "It's the truth. The place was bake-o. I thought I was going to roast under that cap and gown."

Mandy laughed. "Well, you have to tell me all about it."

Tara launched into a funny monologue about the ceremony, leaving out references to the gym.

Steve added a few jokes himself between bites of pizza.

Mandy finally sighed. "Don't you guys have some other parties to go to? I mean—"

Tara grimaced. "Forget it, Mando. You aren't going to get rid of us that easy. We want to be with you."

Mandy blushed. "Oh, you—hey, Brett may come by later."

Tara put her hands to her face. "No way!"

"He called," Mandy offered. "I told him to come by."

Tara let out a girlish shriek. "Oh, that'd be great if you two got back together again."

"Slow down," Mandy replied. "We have to become friends first. I was pretty hard on him."

"He still likes you," Tara insisted. "Oh no! What happens if you both go away to college in the fall? Will it just be a summer fling?"

Mandy took a deep breath. "I'm not going away to school. I'm going to stay here in Port City. I've already applied to the community college."

"Hey," Steve said, "Tara and I are going there, too. All right, we'll be together for another two years!"

Tara screamed gleefully, dancing around the poolside before she tripped and went headlong into the water.

"Come on in," she told Mandy. "It's great."

Mandy stood up on the diving board. She turned quickly, putting her back to the pool, balancing on her toes. She held her breath for a moment, wondering if she could still execute a back flip.

Her legs bent and then sprung upward. Mandy tucked into a ball, spinning around in a neat circle. She opened gracefully, like a blooming summer flower, breaking the surface of the pool with hardly a splash to mark her entrance into the water.

WELCOME TO CENTRAL ACADEMY . . .

It's like any other high school on the outside. But inside, fear stalks the halls—and terror is in a class by itself.

———————————

Please turn the page for a sneak preview of the next TERROR ACADEMY book—don't miss STALKER!

Jody Palmer had been looking forward to the Labor Day celebration at Hampton Way Beach. Her radio alarm blasted rock music at seven o'clock that morning, prompting her to spring up in bed. She turned off the alarm and rose from the soft comfort of her bed, rushing to the window. Her light-blue eyes peered out at the cloudless sky. The sun was climbing over the tops of the maple trees in her back yard, promising a perfect Indian Summer day for Port City and the surrounding New England communities.

A smile spread over Jody's pretty face and she put her hands together. "Yes!" she whispered to herself.

Turning away from the window, Jody studied her reflection in the full-length mirror on the closet door. Her golden blonde hair sprawled carelessly on the frilly shoulders of her nightgown, badly in need of a brushing. She grabbed the hairbrush from her vanity dresser and began to stroke the thick tresses. It was going to be the last fun day of her vacation. All of her friends were gathering at Agony Bluff to say good-bye to summer and hello to the onset of their senior year at Central Academy. They were going to usher in the school year with an old-fashioned picnic and clam bake.

A light tapping on her door preceded her mother's voice. "Jody?"

"I'm up, Mom."

"May I come in?"

"Sure."

Lois Palmer opened the door and eased into her daughter's bedroom. Her eyes were the same light shade of blue as Jody's, and her darker blonde hair had the same golden highlights. Sometimes they were mistaken for sisters. Her mother had the day off from her job at the Port City office of the Indian Head Bank where she served as branch manager. She studied Jody with care.

Jody turned toward her. "What?"

Mrs. Palmer smiled and shook her head. "Oh, I was just wishing that I could get you out of bed so easily on a school day."

"No way," Jody replied.

"Just kidding." She made a face. "Your dad is up. He's in the kitchen fixing pancakes."

Jody grimaced and stuck out her tongue. "Yuk. Alien pancakes from the planet Gag-o."

"They're not that bad," Mrs. Palmer replied.

"Then you can eat mine," Jody offered.

Her mother flashed a comic expression of disgust. "I don't think so!"

They both laughed. Matt Palmer had a reputation as one of Port City's best building contractors, but he was a lousy cook. But they knew they had to humor him when he decided to make breakfast or his feelings would be hurt.

Jody gazed back into the mirror. "I'll be out in a minute."

"Don't worry," Mrs. Palmer said, "you're beautiful. Women pay cosmetic surgeons for noses like yours. You could be a model."

"Sure, and walk up and down a runway like some air head. Forget it. I'm going to be a lawyer or an architect, anything but a model."

Mrs. Palmer's face held a look of concern. "Do you need a ride to the beach, honey?"

"No thanks," Jody replied as she brought her hair into shape, "Sarah is picking me up at eight."

Sarah Martin was Jody's best friend. Sarah already had a car that she had bought during their junior year with the money she saved working at the Pizza Barn in Rochester. Jody still had to complete driver's education before her parents could put her on the family automobile insurance. She hadn't even taken the test for her learner's permit since, unlike most teenagers, Jody didn't care that much about driving.

"Who else is going to be at the clam bake?" her mother asked.

Jody shrugged. "Everyone. Don't worry, Annie Albert's parents are going to be there."

Mrs. Palmer's eyes wandered to the picture of the boy that sat on the vanity dresser. "Is Timothy going?"

A brief flicker of dismay dashed in and out of Jody's irises. "Mom . . ."

"I'm sorry, honey. I was just wondering. He should—"

"Please, Mom, I don't want to think about it. Not today. I want to have a good time."

Mrs. Palmer stepped toward her. "Sure, I understand." She put her hand on Jody's shoulder.

Jody took a deep breath and then sighed. "It's okay, Mom."

They embraced, hugging each other tightly. Mrs. Palmer drew back, frowning. She wished she hadn't brought up the subject, though it seemed healthy to talk about it, at least that was what the psychologist had told them.

"Your father and I could come," she offered. "He wants to take the boat out today, but—"

Jody waved her off. "I told you, it's okay. Forget about it."

Her mother forced a smile. "What are you bringing to the picnic?"

"Steamers," Jody replied. "Sarah and I dug clams yesterday. She kept them in the fridge at her house."

"Are you going to—"

Jody turned away from her, unbuttoning the front of her nightgown. "I have to get ready, Mom. Sarah will be here in a little while."

Mrs. Palmer nodded absently. "Okay. It's just—I love you, honey."

"Mom!"

"Okay, okay."

She started to turn toward the bedroom door.

Jody felt awkward and a little guilty. "Mom?"

"Yes?"

She smiled. "I love you too."

Mrs. Palmer rushed across the room to give her a kiss. "You're a good kid, Jody. We're lucky to have you."

Jody blushed. "I'll be out in a minute. Tell Dad to heat the syrup in the microwave. I can't eat those pancakes unless they're smothered in butter and maple syrup."

"Just thank your lucky stars that he didn't decide to whip up a batch of his famous French toast!"

They laughed again.

Mrs. Palmer left in a hurry, running down the hall. The house was a one-story ranch with a basement. Matt Palmer had built the place in Morningside Groves, a new subdivision on the edge of Prescott Estates, one of the older neighborhoods in Port City. He had designed the house to be energy efficient with all the modern conveniences.

When her mother was gone, the smile left Jody's smooth face. She adored her mother but she wished that Lois Palmer had not brought up such a sensitive subject on this particular day. Her moist eyes focused on the picture of the boy.

She lifted the frame from the vanity, gazing into the soft brown eyes. Timothy had been so handsome before the incident that had changed him. That smiling face would not be attending the Labor Day celebration or any other party for that matter.

Timothy McIntyre had been Jody's first boyfriend. They had gone steady all during middle school. Sarah had been so jealous. Then everything had come down around them. And nothing could change it back the way it had been. After two years, Jody had stopped asking "Why?" At least he was still alive.

"Where did you go, Timothy?"

She replaced the frame on the vanity. With each passing day, Jody found it easier to accept what had happened, but the pain would always be with her to some degree. The hurt would never go away completely. But this was no day to remember sad things from the past. She was determined to have a good time.

Jody's eyes focused on her reflection again. "You're going to make it, Palmer. You hear me? Stay cool."

She turned away from the mirror, busying herself with preparations for the party. She had to get dressed. It was the only way to take her mind off Timothy McIntyre and the tragedy that had haunted their lives.

Jody struck a pose in the archway of the bright, modern kitchen that her parents had designed and decorated together. "Ta-da! Well? How do you like it?"

Her mother looked up from the kitchen table. "Very nice, dear."

Jody was ready for a clam bake at the shore. She wore red and blue flowered shorts over her bathing suit bottom, a white bikini top, a loose, open blouse that matched her shorts and leather sandals. A white visor cap completed the beach ensemble.

"What do you think, Dad?"

Matt Palmer stood in front of the stove, flipping pancakes on a griddle. Her father was a tall, muscular man with thick, sandy hair and a gray-tinged moustache. His rugged face had become tanned from working outdoors in his construction business. The family resemblance was obvious in his blue eyes.

"Dad?" she asked again. "Earth to Dad."

He cast a dubious look in her direction. "Is that all you're going to wear today?"

Jody grimaced, appealing to a higher authority. "Mom?"

"She looks fine, Matt. All the kids dress like that. I approved of the outfit when we bought it."

Jody flexed her arms like a female body builder. "I'm radical, Dad."

"I guess it's okay," he replied in a reluctant voice.

Jody shook her head and stepped across the tile floor to give him a kiss on the cheek. Breakfast in the kitchen made her feel warm, secure and happy. The air smelled of freshly brewed coffee and burnt pancake batter.

"Why don't you go get the paper?" Mr. Palmer asked. "I want to check the tides in the river before we take the boat out."

"No prob," Jody replied.

She left the kitchen, bounding down the hall with the energy of an acrobat. Her spirits soared with the promise of one last day at the beach before school started. Not that she minded going to Central. Jody was a straight-A student and one of the most popular girls in the school. She had been elected to homecoming court in her junior year and many of her friends expected her to be homecoming queen in the fall.

Opening the front door, she strode down the front walk to find the morning newspaper on the perfectly clipped lawn. It had been wrapped in a plastic bag to keep off the dew. Jody picked up the *Port City Press* and then gazed down Brewster Street, a tree-lined thoroughfare that was just waking up to the holiday. Morningside Groves was a great neighborhood, a wonderful place to live. A day like this could even make her forget about Timothy for a while.

She went back into the house and tossed the newspaper on the kitchen table. "This is going to be the most beautiful day of the year," she announced to her parents. "We're going to have a great party."

"Who's chaperoning?" her father asked.

Before she could answer, the phone rang on the

wall. Jody grabbed it. "Hello?" Jody said into the receiver. "It's Annie Albert, Dad. Her mother and father are going to be there. Would you like to talk to them?"

Matt Palmer shrugged. "No, I know Butch Albert. He's an okay guy."

Jody thrust the phone at him. "I'm going to take this in my room. I have to get my beach bag anyway. Hang up when I get there."

He took the receiver from her and rolled his eyes. "Glad to be of service, your highness."

Jody winked at him. "Thanks, Dad."

When she picked up in her room, he hung up and rolled his eyes. "Teenagers and phones. A dangerous combination."

Mrs. Palmer had begun to peruse the front page of the newspaper. "She doesn't talk on the phone that much. Besides, if you don't like it, get her a phone of her own."

"She can have a phone when she can pay the bill," he replied.

"Oh, look. It says here that there won't be any fireworks at the beach this year."

"The city blew the budget on the fourth of July, Lo. This darned recession is hurting everyone. I was lucky to get that contract for the new boat house at the yacht club."

His wife rattled the pages of the paper, scanning the smaller stories at the bottom of the front page. "I think we should—No!"

He looked over her shoulder. "What is it?"

"It can't be! It just can't be!"

"What's wrong, honey?"

She lifted the paper toward his eyes. "See for yourself. It made the front page."

His eyes grew wide as he read the story. "I don't believe it. It's only been two years. They can't—"

"But they are."

"Jody! She doesn't know yet."

She turned to glare at him. "And we're not going to tell her. Not today. Let her go to the picnic."

"Lois! We have to tell her. She's going to find out sooner or later. Man, I don't believe it. This is ridiculous. Two years!"

"Matt—"

"It's better that she knows."

"No, we can't tell her now," Mrs. Palmer insisted. "We just can't tell her—"

"Tell me what?"

They glanced toward the archway of the kitchen. Jody stood there, staring at them. A concerned expression had frozen her pretty face.

Mrs. Palmer folded up the newspaper. "It's nothing, dear." She rose from the table, heading for the recycling bin to throw the paper away.

Jody moved into the kitchen, glancing back and forth between her parents. "What's up?"

Her father smiled weakly. "Uh, it's nothing, honey."

Jody frowned at him. "Something's wrong. I can see it in your eyes."

He turned back to the griddle. "Darn, my pancakes are burning."

"You're keeping something from me," Jody insisted. "I want to know what it is. Tell me."

Mrs. Palmer forced a smile. "It's *nothing*, honey. Just something trivial in the paper."

She stared at her mother. "If it's so trivial, why do you look like you've just seen a ghost?"

"It's the coffee," Mrs. Palmer replied. "It upset my stomach. Your father made it too strong."

"Mom! Tell me what wrong?"

Her father glanced over his shoulder. "Tell her, Lo. Go on."

Mrs. Palmer sighed. "All right. It's about your party, honey. I'm afraid it's going to be spoiled."

Jody frowned. "Spoiled?"

"There aren't going to be any fireworks at Hampton Way Beach this year, honey. Your father and I didn't want to tell you this morning because we know how much you're looking forward to the clam bake."

Jody wasn't ready to believe her. "Get real, Mom."

"That's all, honey. I swear."

Mr. Palmer squinted at his wife with narrow, disapproving eyes. "Lois—"

"I told her!" she snapped back at her husband. "Isn't that enough?"

Jody's face tightened into a grimace. "Is that all? No fireworks."

"Lois—"

"That's all, honey. I hope it doesn't ruin your day."

Jody waved at her. "I knew *that*!"

"You did?"

"Sure," she replied. "The city blew the budget on Independence Day. Everyone knows that. Gah, Mom. You treat me like I'm some kind of baby or something."

"I'm sorry," Mrs. Palmer replied. "It's just that—"

"Lois!" Her father wasn't ready to go along with the ruse. "Jody, I think you better—"

But he never got to speak his mind. A car horn blasted from Brewster Street. It sounded three short bursts and then a long one.

"That's Sarah," Jody said. "She's always early."

Her mother urged her toward the front door. "Go on, honey. You've got a long day ahead of you. Have a good time."

"Thanks, Mom. Bye, Dad."

"What about breakfast?" her father challenged.

"We'll get something on the way," Jody replied. "Later, guys!"

When she was gone, Mr. Palmer took a deep breath and sighed dejectedly. "We should have told her."

"No."

"What if she finds out from someone else?" he said blankly.

Mrs. Palmer eased into her chair. "Let her have one more happy day before she finds out. She's been so together the last six months. Who knows what this will do to her?"

"You think she's strong enough to handle it, Lo?"

Mrs. Palmer put her hands together and bowed her head as if to pray. "I hope so, Matt. I really hope so."

TERROR ACADEMY

Welcome to Central Academy...
It's like any other high school on the outside. But inside,
fear stalks the halls—and terror is in a class by itself.

LIGHTS OUT

When Mandy's father dies suddenly, she fears there's more to this "accident" than meets the eye. Reporting for the school paper, she secretly investigates the shady suspects hidden within Central Academy. But her darkest suspicions lead her to Central's new assistant principal. A man with a question-able past. The man her mother plans to marry...

__ 0-425-13709-0/$3.50

STALKER

Jody Palmer remembered everything about the attack–how could she forget the fight that nearly killed her boyfriend Timothy? It was her testimony that put Bubba Barris behind bars for two years. But now he's out...and he's coming back to Central.

__ 0-425-13814-3/$3.50 (On sale July 1993)

SIXTEEN CANDLES

Kelly Langdon has slimmed down, shaped up, and become one of Central's most popular students! She's finally put her parents' mysterious deaths behind her and come out of her shell. But a killer still stalks her. And now Kelly's next date may be her last....

__ 0-425-13841-0/$3.50 (On sale August 1993)
